RENDEZVOUS AT HELL'S RIM

Hell's Rim is the right name for this territory, all right, Will Rhianon thought as he rode into Coffin Rock in the gray dawn. Huge boulders darkened the town edges and Coffin Rock itself split the main street in two, casting a black shadow on his path.

Rhianon figured he'd get a job done here and move out quickly. But he was known as a mighty fast gun—and was the target for every rep-hungry hothead. He had stripped the marshal's star from his vest, but he couldn't strip away the crimson reputation that followed him.

And before Rhianon could get his kid brother out of trouble, his very presence triggered off an avalanche of hellfire.

CLIFF RIDER

LIN SEARLES

CHARTER
NEW YORK

A DIVISION OF CHARTER COMMUNICATIONS INC.
A GROSSET & DUNLAP COMPANY

CLIFF RIDER
Copyright © 1968 by Ace Books, Inc.

An ACE CHARTER Book

Published simultaneously in Canada

Manufactured in the United States of America
2 4 6 8 0 9 7 5 3 1

I

COFFIN ROCK lay sprawled against the foot of
the rugged escarpment of Hell's Rim, a town without shape and without reason. A brittlely striking
morning sun threw the squat adobe buildings into
harsh relief, their shadows falling across the town's
single street in sharply-angled patterns that to Will
Rhianon seemed all wrong.

Rhianon, coming out upon the Lost Coon
Hotel's weather-faded porch, had the instant feeling that his hard night's ride had brought him to
the end of the world. Hell's Rim lofted its immense
barrier immediately behind the street's farther side,
its towering mass so close that Rhianon had to lift
his head to see the top. Huge boulders, outflung
from some eon-old surge of the earth's crust, somehow hung to the rimrock's steep rise, their bases
eaten away by centuries of eroding winds.

Rhianon brought his gaze back to Coffin Rock's
graceless outlines, his morning cigar still unlit and
his first savor of this day's warm awakening now
turning sour. Across the street the wooden awning
of the Bulldog Saloon was hanging at an awkward
angle, one of its supports lying across the plank

1

walk, the rope that had pulled it down still looped around it. A buckboard lay on its side in front of Horner's Barber Shop next door, one wheel still spinning lazily. Broken glass littered the plank walk, one shard throwing back a challenging answer to the sun's slanted strike against the house-size boulder that split the street in front of Hunstedder's General Store. A turkey buzzard lifted in ungainly flight from behind the boulder, cut that lancing shaft of light and swooped drunkenly towards Hell's Rim.

A voice behind Rhianon said softly, bitterly: "It is a beautiful sight, isn't it?"

He turned then, a gauntly tall man with dark and somber eyes, and swept off his hat. He paused a moment before answering, oddly stirred by something he saw in this girl who spoke to him. She wore a faded gingham dress and her auburn hair was drawn severely back into a prim knot, but her wide-spaced eyes were of the deepest blue and the fine bones of her face made planes that gave her features a lively gentleness. She had, Rhianon thought, something more than beauty—a fineness and a cleanness that made a man's memories turn back to better days.

He had the instant impulse to say something gallant, but there was something in this girl's quietly grave manner that made him change his mind. He said instead, "This is my first look. I rode in before dawn. Do you mean the town or the rim?"

"To me," she answered, "both are frightening."

He gave her a swiftly appraising look. "You're from the east. This is a raw country, but you'll learn someday to live with this land and feel the gentleness of its strength."

"And the men who ride over it?"

"Towns get treed now and then."

He glance dropped and lifted, touching a moment upon the smooth walnut handle of the long-barrelled Peacemaker holstered low at his thigh.

"I have heard the lecture before." Her voice took on overtones so gently ironic that Rhianon was not sure she was serious. "And men must carry guns and sometimes kill. Isn't that the rest of it?"

"I once thought so."

"And now?"

"Times change—people change." The conversation was taking a path Rhianon wished to avoid, and the memory of those days at once so recent and so long ago drew its knife-sharp edge across his thoughts and left its painful impress.

"Ah," she murmured, and gave him a deeply speculative glance. "And now you are going to tell me that guns don't kill people—only people kill people."

"No," he said soberly, and the constrained and tight-lipped way of his speech made a definite closing off of this talk.

"I am sorry," the girl said in a low voice. "I see that I've probed a spot that hurts. It was not my intention."

"Never mind," he said. He raised a hand in a gesture that took in the length of the street. "I was under the impression there was law in this town."

"In name," she replied. "There is a man with a star. The real law is no doubt sleeping it off on the pool table in the Bulldog." Her lips lost their fullness, and to Rhianon's unspoken question she added, "Rhino Colvig. You will no doubt meet him. He makes a point of informing strangers who runs Coffin Rock."

Rhianon shook his head. "I will not be staying long enough." He fought to keep his voice steady, but a sudden surge of strong excitement quickened his pulse. He had thought he could ride into this town, make his secret contact with Miles Brandes, do what he came to do, and ride out again. Now he knew he had guessed wrongly; the mention of Rhino Colvig's name was like the warning whirr of a sidewinder. He thought: *Dodge, Las Vegas, Tombstone, and now here. The dust a man raises along his trail never really settles.*

The girl said, her voice grown cool, "Another fiddle-footed man. Does this country breed any other kind?" She turned swiftly away and went back into the hotel before Rhianon could answer.

Rhianon jammed his flat-crowned hat back upon his head and slipped the almost forgotten cigar into a vest pocket. He thought: *Dammit, how does a man always turn out to be wrong?*

He was uneasily impatient to find Miles Brandes, but knew he would have to hold himself in check, letting Miles make the contact in his own way and in his own time. He had a way, once making a decision like this, of setting it completely aside and turning his thoughts to immediate considerations. At this moment a tightening of his stomach muscles reminded him that he hadn't eaten since early yesterday afternoon, and he wondered where in Coffin Rock he would be able to get breakfast. The Lost Coon Hotel held the dubious distinction of being the largest as well as the only frame building in Coffin Rock, but no meals were served there unless a man wanted to drink his dinner.

Rhianon directed his gaze down the street, his eyes searching for a sign indicating an eating place. His glance touched the swing doors of the Bulldog Saloon, and he frowned and held himself very still, watching the man who was bulling his way through them. He was a man who seemed to be not much larger than a Cheyenne teepee, and was built upon roughly the same lines. He had a florid face and a thick neck, and he wore a gun holstered lower than usual. He came directly across the street in a purposeful spraddle-legged stride, his strangely yellow eyes full upon Rhianon. Behind him the swing doors of the saloon still swung from the force of his passage.

Colvig, Rhianon told himself, *always Colvig. All right, play it soft. Play it easy and cool and soft.* So far, during the dark lonely days since he had laid aside his star, he had avoided trouble. He wondered if he could step away from this, and instantly knew he could not. For Colvig's walk held the rough arrogance of a man not to be put off; his whole body carried a tense threat.

Rhianon expelled a deep breath and hooked a thumb in his gunbelt, this utterly deliberate movement a tacit and neutral acknowledgment of Colvig's presence. He held himself like this, not otherwise moving, until Colvig passed the tie-rail and reached the plank walk fronting the hotel.

Colvig halted there, his big body cocked slightly forward, giving Rhianon the full wickedness of his gaze. He said, in a voice with an undertone of jeering mockery: "The big law. You come to bring peace and light to Coffin Rock?"

Rhianon said gently. "Go back and finish your drinking, Rhino. This town has seen enough for a morning."

Colvig grinned crookedly, strong teeth making a white flash beneath his drooping moustache. "Just come over to give you some friendly advice. We got one lawman here—we don't need another. Make it a short visit."

A quick surge of temper gripped Rhianon, and he fought it off grudgingly. He had learned to form a barrier against these swift swirls of raw anger that sometimes touched him; and he forced himself to take three strides to the walk with a deliberate concentration, taking a long and slow breath with each step.

He said then, "I will stay or leave Coffin Rock at my own pleasure—and I wear no star."

"We'll just have a look," Colvig said abruptly, and with a surprisingly rapid motion yanked Rhianon's vest open.

Rhianon murmured, "Pull it back in place, Rhino."

"I guess not," Colvig said, and his eyes narrowed wickedly. "I heard stories, but I've always had a hankering to see for myself. No, my friend— you don't look that tough any more," and his free hand was already coming up.

Rhianon muttered, "Damn you," and his hand streaked down, coming up again in a short arc, six-gun palmed. He laid the barrel hard upon Colvig's knuckles, then in a motion, utterly swift, utterly sure, whipped it across Colvig's cheekbone. The front sight raked across Colvig's face from ear to mouth; an angry red line traced its crescent brand upon Colvig's heavy features. Colvig's sixgun, half out of its holster, twisted from his stinging fingers and landed hollowly upon the boards. Rhianon kicked it into the street and stepped forward, hearing Colvig's animal cry of pain lifting in high protest. He swung the sixgun again, catching Colvig going down.

Colvig went to his knees then, and stayed there, his breath coming deeply and hoarsely, his head shaking slowly from side to side. A crop of blood splashed into the dust at the walk's edge, making a crimson-pimpled crater at that spot.

Rhianon said, his voice carrying sharp through the early morning quiet, "How many more times, Rhino?"

Colvig's yellow gaze impaled him with a triumphant malice. "I've learned what I wanted to know, my friend. There will be another time."

"You are wrong," Rhianon said, his voice flat. "This is the last time. Get out of my sight, Rhino."

"This time," Colvig said thickly, and came to his feet. He threw a look at the gun lying on the walk, then raised his eyes to meet Rhianon's warning gaze. He shrugged his bulky shoulders, then turned away, saying, "There is always another gun."

Rhianon watched him make his unsteady way downstreet until he was lost from view behind the boulder. He holstered the gun then, picked Colvig's up and thrust it into his waistband. This sudden dark outburst of his temper left him shaken. The incident had not been of his choosing, but he felt no regret—and this knowledge of himself disturbed him more. Thinking thus, he had the sudden realization he was not alone, and he turned to face a spare gray-haired man who stood silently in the hotel's entrance.

The gray-haired man said dryly, "Makes getting up in the morning seem worthwhile. I've been waiting to see that ever since I arrived in Coffin Rock."

Rhianon threw him an irritable glance. "Then why the hell didn't you do it?"

"My name isn't Rhianon," the man said, his voice even. He met Rhianon's sharply inquiring look with a steady gaze, a corner of his mouth lifting slightly under the neatly-trimmed gray moustache. "If you don't want to be known, don't sign hotel registers. Mister, I hope you plan to stay a spell in Coffin Rock. We need somebody like you."

"Passing through," Rhianon said. "I have lost nothing in this town."

"Funny," the man drawled. "Would have thought otherwise. Change your mind, leave word for Colonel Bevins. You'll want to turn in that gun. Marshal's office downstreet—past the Coffin."

Rhianon gave him a puzzled look. "The Coffin?"

"That big rock splitting the street. You can't tell from this angle, but from the side it looks like a big coffin. Town got its name from it. Must have broke loose from the rim a long time ago. Anyway, the street forks there, as you can see, then comes together again past the Coffin's head."

Rhianon's gaze followed Colonel Bevin's wide-gesturing arm. Past the Coffin a swirl of dust rose and lengthened into a drooping plume; a quickening fanfaronade of hooves made a muffled beat upon the morning's flat stillness. That, Rhianon knew, would be Colvig riding out. If things were as they used to be, Colvig would be reporting soon to Pride Qualtrough—and this night would darken with the threat of violence. He hoped he could get his business taken care of and leave before that time came. He watched the dust plume settle behind the Coffin's immense bulk, and he felt his shoulder muscles lose their tautness.

Colonel Bevins said, turning away, "You may change your mind. My daughter told of speaking to you earlier. I think she is wrong." The hotel doors swung shut against his back.

Rhianon took the cigar from his pocket and lit up, giving the street his searching survey. It was still too early for the town's full awakening, but there was a sense of reluctant stirring and the small sounds of early morning made a dissonant rhythm. A pan clattered, and a man's voice, morning-low, rumbled with fervent swearing; a dog set up a steady barking and then broke off suddenly with a shrill yipe; a window shutter on the Lost Coon's second floor banged open. Across the street a man wearing a canvas apron pushed through the bat-wing doors, ran fingers through tousled hair and gazed morosely at the broken glass before lifting his eyes to give Rhianon a curious look. Shrugging his shoulders, he began sweeping the walk in a half-hearted way, as though knowing it would have to be done all over again.

Rhianon, Colvig's gun a hard and uncomfortable pressure upon his belly, left the porch and turned onto the plank walk. Making his way past the Coffin, he laid his attention upon that gigantic boulder and noted how it dwarfed even the solid outline of Hunstedder's store. Past Hunstedder's this western fork of the street angled sharply and then widened where the two forks of the street met. A vacant lot, grown to scrub mesquite and mescal, sided the store's farther side; a jumble of smoke-blackened adobe bricks made a tumbled cairn in its center. Past this point, adobe buildings lined both sides of the street, some of them with wooden awnings. A faded barber pole marked the next building past the vacant lot; Horner's Barber Shop had evidently moved. Next to that, a sign hanging so low that Rhianon had to duck his head advertised a newly whitewashed adobe as the Coffin Saloon.

The saloon swamper came out as Rhianon passed this place and splashed a bucket of water across the walk. He muttered, "Sorry, stranger," and blocked Rhianon's path.

Rhianon said, "Place to eat here?"

The swamper pointed down street. "Two doors past the jail yonder. Should be open now." He threw a quick look behind him and lowered his voice. "Will, he's here, but you won't like it. Elephant Corral, end of the street. Where you left your horse. I'll meet you behind the stables in about an hour."

"Thanks, Miles," Rhianon said, and passed on.

II

THE JAIL was a squat adobe building with flakes of whitewash still showing around the single barred window. A sign beside the door read: *Third Wellington, Town Marshal. Knock!* And below this somebody had penciled in, *Dog Catcher, Fire Bucket Filler, Street Commissioner, Jailer.*

Pausing a moment to read this legend with wry amusement, Rhianon rapped his knuckles against the door. When he got no answer, he took Colvig's gun and banged on the door with the butt.

A man's voice grumbled crossly, "Well, dammit, leave a few splinters for the next man!"

Rhianon shoved the door open and stepped inside to confront a hugely obese man struggling to pull a faded red shirt down over his head. His face was completely hidden, and the strangely misshapen bulge where the top of his head should have been caused Rhianon to stare in disbelief.

Third Wellington's voice came with muffled irritableness through the cloth. "Damned thing must have shrunk."

Rhianon said dryly, "Why don't you try it with your hat off?"

"Done it this way twenty years. You put your shirts on your way, I'll put mine on my way."

"As such," Rhianon murmured, and watched as a final yank brought the shirt down past Wellington's head.

Third Wellington looked at Rhianon with button-black eyes set widely apart by a bulbous nose. The black derby hat seemed too small for his bulk; it sat far above his ears as though glued there. Wellington tapped it, hitched his suspenders over his shoulder, tucked in his shirttail, and eyed Rhianon with a peevish intentness.

"What in hell's the gun for?"

"Found it on the walk," Rhianon answered. "Thought I'd better turn it in." He tossed the gun onto a desk littered with Wanted dodgers and other papers.

"Don't say," Wellington muttered. He stepped to the desk, hefted the gun briefly and dropped it into the drawer. When he raised his eyes to Rhianon again his glance was shrewd and careful. "Looks like Rhino Colvig's iron. He don't just leave it lying around."

"Did this time."

The fat lawman slammed the drawer shut. "You want some advice?"

"No," Rhianon said flatly, and turned away. A thought struck him then as he palmed the door open, and he spoke over his shoulder. "Just this much. Where does a man get breakfast in this town?"

"Shoo-Fly Cafe, few doors down." Wellington scraped a match into life against his derby and lit up a Long Nine. "And I'll give you some advice anyway."

"This has been my day for it," Rhianon said. "All right, make your speech."

"Don't eat their ham," Wellington said glumly.

The Shoo-Fly Cafe squatted drably between a gutted adobe that looked like it had once been a bank and the street's far end at the Elephant Corral. Rhianon wolfed down his steak, eggs, and coffee, slapped a half-dollar into the hand of the sullen oldster who ran the place and left. He needed sleep, but he was far too restless to return to the hotel room besides being afraid he might miss the meeting with Miles Brandes. The presence of Colvig was a disturbing weight upon his thoughts, and he wondered what meaning lay behind this. Colvig and Qualtrough were the kind who preferred the larger towns where they could control the gambling, work their con games on the suckers, and keep a predatory eye upon the bullion shipments. Coffin Rock didn't appear to have much to offer.

Pride Qualtrough had been the guiding genius of the bunch back in the Las Vegas days, with Colvig handling the rough work for him. Rhianon had helped break the bunch up in Vegas. Then Colvig appeared in Tombstone and was kicked out along with the Earps after the murders at the O.K. Corral. But Colvig wouldn't be working alone. Other members of the old Hoodoo bunch would be with him, plus whatever new recruits he might have picked up. And it was the thought of who might be now riding with him that made Rhianon's dark eyebrows draw together.

He shrugged this dark mood aside then, thinking, *That bridge hasn't even been built yet;* and, the morning offering nothing better, stepped past the

Coffin's head to have his look at the other side of
the street. He had long made a habit, upon riding
into a strange town, of making a survey of its angles and shadows, taking mental note of the
places where a man could be ambushed or caught
in a whipsaw. It was this almost automatic
thought, born of long years of carrying the star
into far places, that guided his indolent strides to a
view of the Coffin's other side. He thought, A *sorry
town,* and then came to an abrupt and amazed halt.

For this side of the street between the Coffin and
Hell's Rim was in marked contrast to the run-
down and decayed look of the side he had just left.
He counted four new frame buildings set between
older adobe structures, their raw and unpainted
pine clapboards a startling contrast to the weathered adobe. This side of the street reminded
Rhianon of Dodge City during its busy growing
days. A butcher shop, freight office, and hardware
store were already open; a general air of brisk ex-
pectancy indicated that the rest of the street was
awakening.

Rhianon lit up another cigar, stepped around a
pile of fresh lumber, and made his slow way down
the street's middle dust, puzzling over this until he
found himself in front of the Bulldog Saloon. Here
he cut over past the Coffin's foot to the hotel, finished his cigar upon the veranda of that place, then
walked back to the hardware store.

The sign hanging from the wooden awning read:
Hardware, Guns, Saddlery. J. Spurlock, Prop. A
small man with ragged gray sideburns and eyes like
dirty ice dragged a chair through the door, planted
it beside the oil-papered window, and went back
inside, giving Rhianon a speculative look.

Rhianon pushed through the half-open door, ducking his head, and threaded his way through a heterogeneous gathering of tools, harness, and odd parts. The proprietor had vanished into some other part of the building, and Rhianon wandered aimlessly throughout the store, finally making his way to the gun rack. Here he picked up a Winchester '94, sighted carefully at an Argand lamp, then sighed regretfully and replaced the gun carefully back upon the rack.

He called out then, "Anybody here?"

The man he had seen earlier came from the back room, wrestling a nail keg. He grunted, "With you in a minute," and shoved the keg into a corner. When he again gave Rhianon his attention his eyes were without friendliness.

"They should put wheels on those damn things. What can I do for you?"

"Need a new cylinder pin," Rhianon said.

"Got some somewhere," the man said, and moved over to a cabinet by the gun rack. "New in town, ain't you? I'm Jim Spurlock. Besides being a nail keg wrestler, I'm also mayor of Coffin Rock. Always glad to meet the new settlers. A thriving town, sir, a thriving town. Three months ago it was dying on its feet. Now that they've moved the Apaches to San Carlos and opened the land to resettlement this whole part of the county will be booming. Started already, as you see. What kind of gun?"

"Colt. Army .45," Rhianon replied. He brought two silver dollars from his pocket and placed them on the cabinet.

Spurlock fumbled in a drawer, brought out a cylinder pin. He said, "That will be five dollars."

"A mite steep," Rhianon objected.

"A mite far piece up to Willcox or over to Tombstone, too," Spurlock said flatly. "You want it or not?"

"You make it a little rough for a man to live," Rhianon said. He brought out three more silver dollars, dropped them upon the cabinet and took the cylinder pin from Spurlock.

"Freighting runs high. You going to settle here, you'll have to get used to it."

"Passing through," Rhianon said. "For which I am now thankful." Ignoring Spurlock's resentful look, he drew his colt from leather, pulled the hammer back to half-cock and punched the cartridges out. He moved to a bin of small tools, selected one, and replaced the old cylinder pin with the new one. He was thoroughly aware that Spurlock was giving him an intensely curious scrutiny, but he did not again look at the man until he had finished his chore and dropped the gun back into leather.

He said then in a dry as dust voice, "Charge for using your tools?"

Red crept up to the ragged line of Spurlock's sideburns. His voice was sullen. "No."

"My thanks," Rhianon drawled, and left, feeling Spurlock's raging gaze upon his back.

When he came upon the street he found the town bustling with full awakening. Spring wagons and buggies were parked alongside the Coffin's gray bulk; a group of soberly dressed men talked earnestly in front of the freight office. One of the men threw his arms out in a wide hopeless gesture and stalked away. Farther down the street two riders racked up at the tie-rail in front of Roybal's Butcher Shop and walked diagonally over to the saloon next door. Third Wellington kicked thoughtfully at a water barrel placed beside the Acme Assay Company, noticed Rhianon, and said in a casually neutral voice, "Going to be another hot one."

"My thought," Rhianon answered.

Wellington whipped a bandanna from his hip pocket, pushed back his derby and wiped his forehead. "On my way to the hotel. Heading back in that direction?"

"To the Elephant Corral," Rhianon answered. "Thought to have a look at my horse."

"Hope you'll find him," Wellington said enigmatically and passed on.

Rhianon continued his way down street toward the Elephant Corral, the puzzle of Coffin Rock's revival now becoming more and more clear. The settlement of the Indian lands was bringing in homesteaders and merchants. The nearest other supply points of any size would be Tombstone and Willcox, unless a man elected to risk a long trip to Lordsburg. This part of the street between Hell's Rim and the Coffin would naturally be the first to be built up for it would be shaded throughout the greater part of the day. Coffin Rock could be a bonanza for a man on the make. Rhianon wondered how many of these new businesses had Pride Qualtrough behind them as a silent partner.

The wide doors of the Elephant Corral yawned in front of him. He passed into this shaded wooden cavern, gave the hostler a casual salute, and said, "My black in a stall?"

"Rear, on the right," the hostler said. "Riding out?"

"Just want to have a look."

The hostler turned his head and called out, "Slim! Man coming to take a look at his horse."

"I'll show him," Miles Brandes' voice called back. "Straight back, mister."

This far end of the Elephant Corral's shed lay in half-darkness. Rhianon paused beside a pile of grain sacks, the dimness making him unsure. He heard soft footfalls upon the tanbark's soft dampness. He turned that way and saw a tall shadow, made shapeless by the stable's angles, pull away from one of the farther box stalls. In a moment the lanky figure of Miles Brandes loomed beside him.

"This way," Brandes murmured, and led him to the sable darkness of the stable's far corner.

Rhianon reached out and put a hand upon the black's withers and said, "Just me, boy."

Miles Brandes said, "I can't give you all of it now. The joker in front will be wondering why I'm not pitching manure."

"Whatever you can," Rhianon said quietly.

"The kid is here," Brandes said. "I came in, got a part-time job sweeping the saloon, another one here. Saw him the second day. He's going by the name of Johnny Minstrel. Now why that, I wonder?"

"Easy enough," said Rhianon. "My mother's name."

"So," Brandes murmured. "Anyway, he didn't recognize me. I've had a drink or two with him. He's riding with Qualtrough and Colvig. You've already seen Colvig—the leaves have been rustling this morning. Far as I can figure, nobody knows he's your brother. Will, I do wish you had come into Coffin Rock more quiet-like."

"It was a fool thing," Rhianon said slowly. "But

it's too late for second-guessing. I've got to talk to him and get him away from here."

"Take some doing," Brandes said thoughtfully.

"My chore now," Rhianon said. "You've done everything a man can ask a friend to do—and more." He reached out and gripped Brandes' shoulder.

Brandes shook his head. "No. Give me a few days. I've talked to him some. Give me a chance to get closer. He's been asking if I'd like to work for Qualtrough. Maybe I can get to him through that. Perhaps even tonight. You and Johnny and me will be starting that horse-wrangling business yet. I'll leave word at the hotel."

Rhianon said, sober-voiced, "No damn-fool tricks, now, Miles."

"Don't worry," said Miles Brandes, and vanished into the stable's farther darkness.

Again into the street's morning light, Rhianon kept to the Coffin's western side, walking slowly back to the hotel. As he passed the jail's open door, Third Wellington stepped out and said in an aggrieved tone, "Stopped in at the hotel. You didn't tell me who you were."

"Didn't ask," Rhianon said.

"Old age," Wellington said. "Makes a man forgetful. Point is, this town has enough problems as of now. Colvig will be riding back before sundown. Most likely with a few guns behind him. I would take it a kindness were you to leave Coffin Rock before that time."

III

THERE WAS A TIME, Rhianon knew, when no man would have asked him to leave a town—even in terms as carefully phrased and politely couched as Third Wellington's. That had been a thousand years ago when the trails were young and his star was bright in the eyes of the violent men who looked upon it. For a brief moment the memory of that older time gripped him and had its way with him; and the sun hung crimson in the dust of a thousand trail herds, and the plank walks resounded with the trampling of Texas boots and the jangle of spur chains. And Will Rhianon, a tall man on a tall horse, breasted this hard-surging tide and halted it and brought it to order.

A vagrant dust devil swirled out of some obscure place to ripple his shirt and make a dryness in his nostrils. The vision passed away, and he looked through its fading mist to see Third Wellington patiently awaiting his answer.

He said, "What happened this morning was not of my seeking."

"Happened, though," Wellington said. "You know Colvig won't let this one pass."

Rhianon said, "I've business that makes it important I stay here a while." He let out a gusty breath
then and asked a thing he had never asked before.
"Will Colvig accept an apology?"

Wellington shot him a glance that was sharp and
sad and disbelieving. "Sounds doubtful. We can
work on it."

"It would be a favor," Rhianon said slowly. He
resumed his course toward the hotel.

Third Wellington said, "Not so damned fast.
Stay in the hotel until you hear from me. The bar
is all right—none of the bunch come in there. And
I'm damned if I know why I'm doing this."

Rhianon turned abruptly. "Why are you?"

Wellington swiped his face with his bandanna.
"I think you were the kind of lawman I always
hoped I might have been."

"And now?" Rhianon said bluntly.

"Never mind now." Wellington stuffed the bandanna into a hip pocket. "Just kind of hole yourself up in that hotel, will you?"

The Lost Coon Hotel was a dried out frame
building that had once been painted white and
looked as though it had given up caring. The
veranda held three battered wooden rockers, and
an ocotillo had somehow pushed itself up between
a couple of loose boards. In the lobby two rows of
hard straight chairs faced each other over a strip of
worn carpet. At one side double doors let into the
bar. Back in the dimness was a desk, and beyond
this a flight of unsteady-looking stairs angled upward to the rooms above.

Nobody was at the desk. Rhianon reached
across it, picked his key from a nail and went up-

stairs. The girl who talked to him this morning passed him in the hall, gave him a curious look, and went on without speaking. Once in his room, his door left open to help make a draft, he sat on the edge of the bed and stared at his boots until the long night's ride without sleep caught up with him.

He dreamed the same dream that had night after night claimed his resting hours, living over again that painful and horror-stricken moment when he looked over the smoking muzzle of his gun and saw the child sprawled upon the dust of Fremont Street and the blood staining the blue plaid dress of the doll she still clutched. It was always the same, even to the way one pigtail with its red ribbon at the end had fallen over her eyes.

There must have been more, he knew, but this was always where the dream stopped.

He had tried before that incident to control the whiplash reflexes that long years of carrying a gun and a star had given him. When Johnny first came from Iowa to work with him, he spent hours cautioning him about shooting before thinking. And after Johnny got tired of walking in his shadow and left he gave the same lesson to the other young men who felt it an honor to follow his bright star.

Then in one brief moment his star was crimson.

The inquest exonerated him in the eyes of everybody but himself. Others were shooting; the street was heavy with a leaden hail; there was no certainty that the shot was his. He tried to convince himself of this, but the deeper and darker recesses of his mind had their way with him. Both the gun and the star became weights he could not bear. He turned the star in one day in mid-October. But he was no foolish idealist. In this country he would be soon dead without the gun. So he wore it, a deadly steel albatross strapped to his thigh. And he knew he would have to wear it and fight it until he found Johnny Minstrel.

He awoke with his shirt wetly plastered to him and sweat beading the lines of his square jawbones. The room was still and hot; somehow the door had swung shut. From the window he could see the distant peaks of the Chiricahuas, and southward the purpled rise of the Pedregosa range. Coffin Rock, he realized now, must lie near the northern tip of the Peloncillos in that vaguely indeterminable area where the San Simon and San Bernardino valleys joined. He stared from the window while a wedge of sunlight fell off the corner of the washstand and slipped noiselessly to the floor. He splashed water on his face, combed his hair back, and put on a clean shirt. He was buckling his gunbelt when knuckles rapped the door and Third Wellington entered without waiting for an answer.

Wellington's derby was pushed back, exposing a completely bald pate; his button eyes held some troubled thought. His huge belly overlapped the front of his gunbelt, completely hiding it. He made an ineffectual hitch at the belt, gave it up and looked at Rhianon with a morose regard.

"You still want to play it that way?"

"Never did," Rhianon said. "But I'll play it any way that will let me stay here long enough to get my business done—and no trouble."

The undulating echoes of a shot bounced from the Rim and drifted through the window. Immediately upon the wake of this sound came somebody's shrill, "Eeeyah!"

Wellington stepped to the window and peered out. "Wrong side for a look-see," he muttered, and turned again to face Rhianon. "Colvig and a bunch of the boys are here."

Rhianon said, "Talked to him?"

Wellington shook his head. "No. Wanted to see you again first." He sighed hugely, yanked out his bandanna and mopped his neck. "I was hoping Qualtrough would show, but he's still in Lordsburg talking to the railroad people. Whatever you think of him, he'd make Colvig listen to reason. He wants to give the railroad the image of Coffin Rock as a nice and peaceful and prosperous town."

"I'm impressed," Rhianon drawled.

Wellington threw him a hurt look. "I do my best. Anyway, when Qualtrough is away, Colvig and his guns run pretty much roughshod through Coffin Rock. I'm not a damn bit sure how he'd auger this play. And a hell of a lot less sure I could stop anything he decided to do."

Rhianon said soberly, "If this is putting you too much in the middle—"

"I'm always in the middle," Wellington cut in. "This here now business of yours pretty important?"

"More than I could tell you."

Wellington said, "Ah," and gave him a long look. "You know Rhino Colvig as good as I do. You know what he'll want you to do."

"Crawl," Rhianon stated flatly.

"Will you crawl?"

"If it will buy me enough time to finish what I came here for."

Wellington let out a long breath. "All right—I'll try. Come down with me. Stay in the lobby. Maybe we can at least make a truce until tomorrow. Qualtrough should be back then. He won't like you being here, but he'll have some of the railroad big augers with him and he won't want any trouble."

A heavy sound of galloping hooves drifted in from the street. A man's laughter lifted in raucous mockery, high and wickedly pitched. Yellow dust floated past the window, defied gravity there for a moment's span and then fell away.

"Fool time has started," Wellington muttered. "Better get on this before they're all roostered."

The stairs shook under Third Wellington's heavy stride. Rhianon, following, felt as though he were trailing a small earthquake. As they reached the desk the hotel's front doors flew open and Colonel Bevins, hatless and dust-covered, burst through them. His eyes were wild with a horrified disbelief; his chest was rising and falling with harsh breathing. He gripped Wellington's arm, not seeing Rhianon.

"For God's sake, man! Get out there and stop that!"

Wellington said calmly, "Get hold of yourself, Colonel."

Bevins turned to Rhianon, seeing him for the first time. "You see why we need you? They've dragged that man around the Coffin twice. I tried to stop it. I couldn't. Damn it, somebody's got to stop them!"

Rhianon pushed past them, hearing Third Wellington say, "Boys most likely are having a little fun," and came out upon the veranda. A small knot of men stood across the street in front of the Bulldog Saloon, watching silently. The rider came into view opposite Hunstedder's, hat in hand and spurs raking. A rope was tied to his saddle-horn. Something shapeless and limp dragged in the street at the end of the rope's taut length.

Rhianon vaulted the tie-rail, hit the street in a loose crouch. He realized at once that his timing was wrong; the rider had time to veer to the outside. He made a quick feint in that direction, saw the rider veer that way, then made his lunge as the hoof-thunder became a roar in his ears. He gripped the bridle's cheek strap with both hands and felt his legs yanked out straight from under. Every muscle seemed to stretch to an unbearable tautness. He let himself go slack, making his body into a completely dead weight, and felt the horse's head come down and its stride falter and slow.

The rider yelled something unintelligible, kicked a foot free of the stirrup and aimed a heel at Rhianon's shoulder. Rhianon swung under this, bringing the horse's head farther down. He got his feet back under him then, jerked the horse to a complete halt and grabbed at the rider's leg, missing the ankle but getting the bootheel. He immediately swung his other hand to the man's knee, stiffened that leg and shoved violently upward. He watched the man plummet out of the saddle, arms and legs flailing wildly.

The horse's drive had taken them past the hotel. He said, "Easy, boy," and noticed that the knot of men in front of the Bulldog was drifting apart. He slipped the rope from the saddle-horn, hearing Third Wellington's voice, seeming to come from a long distance away, say, "Just hold it where you are boys." The rider still lay motionless in the dust. Rhianon gave him the briefest look, then followed the rope's slack line back to the man tied to its end.

Colonel Bevins and Third Wellington were already there. Wellington had picked up a shotgun from somewhere; he stood loosely facing the men grouped in front of the Bulldog Saloon. Colonel Bevins, kneeling beside the man, looked up as Rhianon approached.

Rhianon came up slowly. Every step was an effort; every muscle and tendon in his body felt wrenched and torn. He could not seem to draw enough air into his lungs, and it was a distinct effort to speak.

He said finally, "Dead?"

"Not quite," Bevins answered. "I've seen the man around, but I don't know him." He turned the man's face gently upward.

Rhianon looked down into the bruised and bleeding face of Miles Brandes.

IV

RHIANON STARED down upon the broken shape of Miles Brandes, emotions so rapidly crowding his consciousness that all logical thought was pushed aside. He knelt beside Brandes; he put a finger to a corner of Brandes' mouth and swiped away a streak of blood. He looked dumbly at his crimson-smeared finger as though trying to find some meaning in this. Then he came slowly to his feet.

Colonel Bevins said softly: "Rhianon—all right, all right."

"Sure," Rhianon said thickly, "it's all right." He threw a narrow-lidded look across the street, and his next words were flung out harsh and biting. "The sons-of-bitches. The goddam sons-of bitches."

Bevins said, "Seven or eight of them over there."

Third Wellington came over then, sweat making his face glisten. He swung the shotgun in a pointing gesture, and said, "That joker you threw off the horse. He ain't got up yet."

Rhianon said, "You've got a jail, haven't you?"

Wellington looked uncomfortable. He cast a furtive glance at the man standing watchfully in

28

front of the Bulldog Saloon. "Well, now, maybe we ought to consider the whys and wherefores."

"Haul him off," Rhianon said savagely, "or I'll do it for you." He turned to give his full attention to Bevins. "There's got to be a doctor somewhere."

"Not in town," Bevins said. "We've one at the settlement. Best to take him there." And as he spoke, a spring wagon clattered around the Coffin's foot and pulled up squarely in the street's center, cutting off Colvig's bunch.

Rhianon said, "Now, I'll be damned." For the driver of the wagon was the girl he had talked with earlier. Although his mood was utterly black, he could not repress the surge of admiration that rushed through him. This girl's direct action took thinking and courage. She had foreseen the need for the wagon, and then brought it up to the exact spot where it would make the most effective barrier to the threat of violence that lay sullenly explosive in the dust of this troubled street.

Bevins, shaking his head in a wondering way, said to the girl, "Lawney, this is one of those places angels fear to tread."

"Enough fools here at the moment," Lawney Bevins said. She held herself straight and unyielding in the wagon's seat, all of her attention fully directed to Rhianon and her father.

Rhianon said, "Miss Bevins, I admire your courage but I misdoubt your judgment. Your wagon blocks my view. If you would be so kind—"

Colonel Bevins dropped a hand to Rhianon's shoulder, saying mildly, "You're wasting your time. Bevins women have a scandalous amount of stubbornness in them. And your friend needs the doctor. Let's get him there."

Rhianon let out a long breath, his anger draining out with that simple action and leaving him oddly relaxed. Without waiting for help from Bevins, he picked up Miles Brandes and carried him to the wagon.

Lawney Bevins said, "A good two hours ride and a rough trail."

She laid her steady gaze upon Rhianon; the intent of her words was unmistakable.

Rhianon said, "I'll catch up. Wellington will need some help."

Colonel Bevins said, "I can ride with him," and climbed into the wagon bed. He met his daughter's questioning look and added, "He is right in this."

Rhianon said, "Make it a soft ride," and his voice was barely audible. He turned away then, heard Lawney's small *cluck* to the horse, and the slap of reins, and strode over to Third Wellington.

Wellington was bent over the still figure of the rider, swearing softly. As the spring wagon pulled away, he shifted heavily to peer across the street. Colvig's bunch still stood there, an intently watchful group of men, all of them with hands brushing gunbutts.

Rhianon eyed them for the space of a second, then said, "To the jail, Marshal."

"Bastard won't stand," Wellington muttered.

"Drag him, then."

"On a hot day like this," Wellington complained. "Dammit, I can't drag him and watch that mob of gunslingers too."

"I'll watch them."

"Qualtrough will spring him out tomorrow, anyway," said Wellington. He stared peevishly down at the unconscious man, tilted the derby back with the muzzle of the shotgun, and wiped sweat from his forehead with his shirt sleeve. "Linus Pauncefoote! Now ain't that a helluva name for a cheap gunslinger?"

"Get going," Rhianon said. He wheeled and started across the street toward the Bulldog, his deliberate strides sending up little puffs of yellow dust around his boot tops. He saw Rhino Colvig slice the air with abrupt gestures; he saw men break away and fan out along the board walk. He held them at the periphery of his vision, making mental note of their positions, but not taking his attention from Colvig's hugely arrogant shape.

Johnny Minstrel, rising late, somehow managed to make his way to the cook shack without running into anything smaller than the corner of the pole corral. The thought of food made his stomach turn over, but he had a headache built for an elephant, his mouth tasted like the floor of an Apache wickiup, and he felt that any punishment would make him feel better than he felt this moment.

The shack was empty, but a stack of flapjacks squatted coldly at one corner of the table and coffee was still heating in the pot. He squinted his eyes and shuddered at the thought of the flapjacks, but the coffee held his interest a moment. He walked past it, however, rummaged among the cans on the shelves until he found the baking soda, and managed to steady his hand enough to pour some of it into a tin cup. After he poured a dipper of water into the cup and drank the mixture down, holding his nose, he still wasn't sure he felt any better; it took two cups of scalding hot coffee to make his head feel a part of his body again.

While he was pouring a third cup, the door grated open and he turned to see Linus Pauncefoote saunter in. Pauncefoote was a man Johnny Minstrel could never take a liking to. He had a wiry frame without any honest hardness to it, a thin face with a pinched look, and his eyes had stared into the muzzles of too many guns.

Pauncefoote said, "Large night," and made for the stove.

"No truer words," Johnny Minstrel replied. He gulped down more coffee. He set the empty cup down, wiped his mouth with the back of his hand. "Nobody else around?"

"Poker game started in the other shack," Pauncefoote said. "Colvig never has rode back from town. He was trying to rope the Coffin the last I saw him. Never got a big enough loop."

Johnny Minstrel yanked the door open and squinted at the sun. "Getting toward noon. He'll be riding in looking for a dog to kick." He unholstered his sixgun, thumbed the hammer back to half-cock, and twirled the cylinder.

Pauncefoote said, "Better let your head shrink back to normal before you start shooting holes in tin cans. Don't you ever get enough of practice?"

"Not yet awhile," Johnny Minstrel said. He let the hammer ease forward, settled the gun in its holster, and went out the door.

He spent an hour in the box canyon, drawing and firing. Even though he started out shakily, his head bursting with each shot, his draw was still smooth and slick, his aim still accurate. When he finished this session, he dropped his gun back into its leather with a sort of grim exultation; he knew that drunk or sober he could outdraw and out-shoot any man who wore a gun.

Including the one man he wanted most to beat.

He rode back at a high lope, feeling mettlesome and full of juices, his hangover gone, and the thought coming to him that now was the time to light a shuck and look for a job of work where his talents wouldn't be wasted. He never like Qualtrough and Colvig much, anyway. Besides, the whole bunch still treated him like a kid because he didn't have any notches carved into the walnut handle of his gun.

Well, now was the time to cut loose. Nobody here in Coffin Rock worth drawing against. Maybe head for Tombstone. Some good guns there. A fast man could make a reputation. The Earps were gone, but there were still others. Ringo, Buckskin Frank Leslie, Claibourne, a few more Clantons. Get a couple of the good ones, maybe have a law badge offered. Then afterwards let people know your real name. But you'll have done it on your own—not by climbing up your big brother's shirt-tail.

Johnny Minstrel reined up at the corral and re-flectively stroked his upper lip. A man might even grow one of them big droopy moustaches.

He unsaddled, still caught up in high bravery of this better world, turned his horse into the corral, and thudded back to earth when he heard a hard-racking tattoo of hoofbeats and turned to see Rhino Colvig pull up roughly behind him.

One quick look at Colvig was enough, and Johnny Minstrel wisely swallowed the mocking greeting that was at the tip of his tongue. For Colvig was in the blackest of moods. His eyes were red-rimmed and wild; a long and ugly-looking red streak slanted along one entire side of his face, and there was no gun in his holster.

Colvig threw his weight onto the near stirrup and swung heavily down, saying in a taut voice, "Hold still, you goddam brute."

Johnny Minstrel said quickly, "I'll take care of him."

Colvig threw him a look as if seeing him for the first time. "I can damn well take care of my own horse, kid." He unbuckled cinch straps, yanked saddle and blanket off viciously, whipped off the bridle, and booted the horse into the corral. He turned then and gave Johnny Minstrel a calculating scrutiny, his eyes turning crafty.

"Kid, you still looking to carve a notch on that hogleg?"

"Only if it means something," Johnny Minstrel replied.

"It will mean something," Colvig said. "You're looking for a gun rep, you can have it."

Johnny Minstrel said, "When?"

"Before sundown. We're riding back into Coffin Rock. There will be me and a few of the boys, but it will be your play."

Johnny Minstrel said quietly, "Who's the man?"

Colvig gave him a tight grin. "Kid—you wouldn't believe me if I told you!"

Rhianon, his measured strides bringing him closer to Colvig and the pack of gunmen, had the uncomfortable feeling that somehow the pattern was all wrong. The men who broke away from the edges of the group had not drifted off far enough to set up a whipsaw. He saw one man wheel suddenly and pass into the saloon, throwing a nervous look across the street before the batwing doors pushed the shadows around him. This was the hostler at the Elephant Corral, and Rhianon thought: *This is why they picked Miles. One of the gang—and he knew Miles and I weren't talking about horses.*

That left six in the play, counting Colvig. The skinny one and the one with the full beard to the left; the one with the black patch over one eye moving along the boards to the left, this one followed slowly by the one with the wrinkled face. And Colvig, standing stolidly immediately to his front, a smaller and slighter figure half hidden behind him.

He came to a halt about catch-rope distance from Colvig, measuring his angles nicely with the quick perception gained from over a dozen gunsmoke-filled years. The men fanned out along the walk were still within the periphery of his vision; Colvig was a solid target to his front.

He said, "Rhino—this party your idea?" And as his voice ran hard and cool across the air's heavy quiet, he saw the man behind Colvig jerk his head and stiffen his body to bowstring tautness.

The man with the black eye-patch made a small movement. Somewhere behind Rhianon there was a rolling click of a gun hammer thumbed back, and Third Wellington cleared his throat in a rumbling warning.

Colvig said, "Just having a little fun—weren't we, Johnny?" and stepped aside.

V

DARKNESS PRESSED in upon the wide sweep of Rhianon's vision, narrowing the angle until there was only this gun-sight-sharp strip of burning space and the slim-straight shape of the man at the other end of it.

Rhianon felt the incredulous seconds pulse past, and thought: *I should have known*.

He heard Colvig's voice, as from a far distance, say, "Wellington, ain't you slightly mixed up?"

"Just dropped my slice of bread," Third Wellington said. "Always falls butter-side down."

Rhianon looked steadily into the dollar-round eyes of Johnny Minstrel, probing past the layer of sullen surprise and fugitive darkness.

"Kid," he said softly, "did you know who you would be bracing?"

"Wouldn't have made any difference," Johnny Minstrel said. He lifted his head defiantly, his eyes changed and took on stubborn lights; but he shifted his stance uneasily and he held his hand stiffly away from his gun.

Rhianon flicked a sharp look at Colvig. "Rhino, did you think you can always find suckers to do your fighting for you?"

"Talk with your gun," Colvig answered. "You always have before."

Third Wellington's rumbling voice reached over Rhianon's shoulder. "No gun talk. Dammit, how many times I got to tell you no gun talk?"

Rhianon said, "Wellington, just you keep those other boys good Indians." He watched a bottle-fly zoom from the saloon's interior, circle Colvig's head twice and then settle on the man's slashed cheekbone—Colvig's strained effort to avoid making a sudden movement affording Rhianon a moment's wicked pleasure. "Rhino, the kid doing your talking for you?"

"This time," Colvig answered, and sagged visibly as the fly buzzed away.

"In that case," Rhianon said evenly, "let's have your gun, kid."

"I guess not," Johnny Minstrel said, and moved backward a step.

"Why, now," Rhianon murmured, "then I'll have to take it, won't I?"

He moved forward in slow, even strides, his shoulders never losing their level set, his arms swinging loosely like pendulums of some relentless clock that timed only the dark moments of death. This was the way he came toward Johnny Minstrel, as he had a hundred times before to a hundred other men with fingers clawed over their sixguns. He was fully aware of the effect created by this slow march forward, for it was a thing he had studiously worked on and developed; this was a technique of his calling, an action as smoothly professional as the rhythmical anvil blows of a blacksmith.

But never before had he thought he would come toward his own brother in this manner.

Johnny Minstrel, after that first involuntary backward step, said, "Will, it won't work on me." But the blood had drained from his face, leaving his eyes stark and staring from a countenance that seemed to have all its features washed away.

Rhianon said, "Reach easy and drop it, kid," and his last strides overran his voice.

Rhino Colvig said, "Draw, Johnny—draw!"

Rhianon said gently, "You can't do it, can you, Johnny?" He was only two paces from Johnny Minstrel now, but he did not check his measured stride, coming on as though nothing stood before him.

Johnny Minstrel moved back awkwardly, spur rowels grating along the planking. The saloon front stopped him, and he stood there with his back plastered against the clapboards. He breathed raggedly through his mouth. His chest rose and fell in an uneven rhythm that seemed to have no relation to his breathing. He was a man pushed, Rhianon now realized suddenly, to a point beyond that of breaking.

"God damn you!" Johnny Minstrel cried, and his gun hand swept downward. "God everlastingly damn you!"

At Coffin Rock's northern edge where the town petered out among the sorry cairns of tumbled adobe bricks, Lawney Bevins pulled up and handed the reins to her father.

"I can take better care of him," she said.

"Stretched a blanket over for shade," Colonel

Bevins said. "Not much more either of us can do until we get him to Doc Feathers."

"Take the reins, Father," Lawney Bevins said firmly. "You're no longer leading a regiment."

Bevins raised an eyebrow. "Florence Nightingale?" he said in a gently ironic voice, but he climbed over to the driver's seat.

Lawney steadied herself with one hand on the dashboard, hiked up her skirts in a way that to Colonel Bevins seemed wantonly unladylike, and seemed to float down to the road in a billowing cloud of calico.

She said, "Could you see back?"

"Some," Bevins answered. "Rhianon was walking across the street. Thought Wellington was coming along behind him, but I'm not sure of that. I'm thinking I should have stayed."

Lawney shook her head vigorously. "Why? This was not our fight."

Bevins looked down at her, his heavy gray eyebrows drawn together. "Who," he asked dryly, "drove the wagon into the middle of it?"

"Another matter entirely," Lawney answered calmly. She looked into the wagon bed and gave the limply sprawled shape of the man there her full attention.

"Don't worry," Bevins said. "He'll be along soon."

"He is very nice looking," Lawney murmured, not looking away.

"Which one do you mean?" Bevins said in a puzzled tone.

The shot came then, its hard echoes rolling out to them from the town's confines, its sharper tone dulled against the Coffin's immense barrier.

Bevins and Lawney both froze, staring silently at one another.

"Only one," Bevins finally said.

"One shot, one man dead," Lawney said. "Will it help this one here?" She turned away, not waiting for an answer, and lifted herself into the wagon. Miles Brandes opened his eyes briefly, staring blindly and bitterly at some dismal world only he could see. He had this one unwanted moment of consciousness; then he said very clearly, "Ah, no," and went back into the darkness.

Lawney said, "Now, now," and adjusted the blanket that shielded Brandes' face from the sun's wide-slanting burn. She dampened a handkerchief in the water keg and bathed the blood from Brandes' face.

She said to her father, "Never mind the bumps. He won't notice them," and settled Brandes' head in her lap as Bevins reined the team into motion. She cradled Brandes, bracing her back against the side of the wagon, absorbing the jolts, and with a sort of detached interest watched the sun-reddened barrier of Hell's Rim slope downward and lose itself in the flattened reaches of the San Simon Valley.

She realized suddenly that the wagon had halted. She lifted her head sharply and said, "Something wrong?"

Colonel Bevins turned in the seat and looked down at her. "This is the turn-off. He wouldn't know which way to go."

She shook her head. "His friend will know enough to follow the wagon tracks." She gave her father a long doubtful look. "If he comes."

"He'll come," Bevins said, and flicked the reins.

"How do you know that?"

"He's Rhianon," Bevins said, and turned his attention to his driving.

Lawney Bevins pondered this last remark of her father's during the next mile of road, wondering what perverse quirk in men's thinking caused them to make a hero of a man whose only talent was in drawing and firing a gun faster than anybody else. Yet, she thought, this Will Rhianon had a look about him that hinted of more capable things. Just what these other and better things were, she wasn't sure. She tried visualizing him as a farmer, a merchant, a banker—all the solid and safe professions she had looked upon with respect all her life. For a few wild moments she tried to visualize him as a minister, but although she was able to turn his collar around she wasn't able to get rid of the gun strapped to his side.

She tightened her lips and gave her attention to the injured man, but the thought of Rhianon was still a strong pressure upon her even as she looked back along the road and saw the sun-crimsoned plume of dust racing toward the wagon.

There was no easy way to tell at this distance who the rider might be. It could be Rhianon, or it could be one of the Colvig bunch coming to finish the job started in Coffin Rock. And for a few seconds she was shocked to realize she had the unworthy wish that she had a gun.

Her father turned in the seat; gave one quick look, and called, "Whoa! Whoa, now!"

Then the rider hit a stretch of hardpan. The dust

plume fell away and the rider came out of it. He was a tall shape, lean and saddle-whipped, on the back of a coal-black horse; his wide-brimmed hat was pulled low over his eyes, the day's last dusky shadows hid his features and bled away all detail of his somber clothing. Only the ivory butt of the gun at his side was a definite spot of hard clear brightness.

It was not until he reined up abreast of the wagon that the shadows seemed to fall away from him; the sun's waning light slanted across his face, highlighting the square planes of his high cheekbones and the definite shelving of his jaw. He pushed his hat back, and his eyes, darker and softer than Lawney remembered, went straight to the wagon bed.

"How is he?"

"Living," Lawney Bevins said, and threw the blanket back. "Living, but hurt bad."

He guided the black over to the wagon until the stirrup brushed the sideboard. "How long a ride to the doctor?"

Colonel Bevins said, "About three hours, by wagon road. There's a cut-off over the lower slope of Hell's Rim, but a wagon can't make it."

"I can make it, and have the doctor back with him in an hour."

Bevins shook his head. "Rhianon, it's getting dark, and you don't know the trail. Let me have your horse. You and Lawney keep on the road. We'll meet you." He wrapped the reins around the whip socket and climbed down from the seat.

Rhianon slid from the saddle. "Colonel, I find myself beholden to you."

"You may have a chance to repay," Bevins said, and threw a leg over the black. He grunted, and said, "Good horse, this," and was presently lost in the soft folds of the night's gather.

Rhianon listened a moment to the diminishing echoes of the black's hoofbeats, then took the reins of the wagon. He laid one long look upon Lawney Bevins before the gray dusk thickened and darkened and the road became a faint trace between bordering shadows.

Her voice floated up to him, a gentle melody that overlay the creaking of wagon springs and the hard strike of hooves.

"This man—this man here. He is a friend of yours?"

"Yes."

"Then you weren't just passing through Coffin Rock. You came with a purpose."

He tried to evade the question without rudeness. "Purpose to everything a man does, whether it is clear to him or not."

Her voice was steady; it was insistent. "Clear enough for you to send a friend to Coffin Rock to spy out something for you. Clear enough for somebody else to want to kill him." She was silent a few seconds, then added in a more gentle tone. "Have you spent all of your life living within yourself?"

His reply was careful and constrained. "Usually found it best."

"You're lonely," she said slowly. "You're lonely and hurt, and you're going to keep it all roped up inside you because of some stupid and prideful code men have invented. And someday the rope will fray and break."

"What then?" he asked, and found himself oddly straining to hear her answer.

"Never mind," she said wearily, and changed the subject. "We heard the shot. We wondered."

"Whether I killed another man?"

"Yes," she said calmly.

"It's something I don't care to talk about now," he said, and the manner of his speaking, as well as his words, made a flat and definite end to the conversation.

The road ran on, following the indistinct trace of Hell's Rim, angling gently eastward to the vague flatness where the valley met San Simon. It was full night now; starlight made a hazy glow over the rugged peaks of the Pedregosas and the lesser rise of the Peloncillos. A moon and tired silver hung over the land's far darkness. It had the dully bright glint of a gun muzzle.

Rhianon let the horses have their heads, his thoughts straying and focusing on the surprised look on his brother's face as he sank to the boards in front of the Bulldog Saloon, and how the blue spiral of gunsmoke oddly curled and drifted over his head like a ghostly halo.

Thus thinking, and with all sense of time lost, it took a sharp exclamation from Lawney Bevins to make him realize they were being hailed. He pulled up, hearing the colonel's voice rolling toward them along the road's shadowed trace. He called out, "Here, Colonel," and presently saw the two riders emerge from the darkness.

Bevins, wasting no time, said, "In the wagon, Doc," and a coal oil lantern flickered smokily and then settled to a steady orange glow. The wagon

springs creaked. Rhianon turned in the seat to see
Lawney Bevins come to her feet and give a hand to
the man clambering over the tailboard. Then he realized Colonel Bevins was standing by the front
wheel.

Bevins said in a low voice, "If anybody can help
your friend, it's Doc Feathers."

Rhianon said, "Colonel, I didn't think there
were any good Samaritans left in this world." He
wanted to say more, but the words would not
come.

Lawney Bevins, behind him, said softly, "You
were right, Mr. Rhianon. There are none. Just people who think a man's life is an important thing."

Before Rhianon could wholly gauge the deeper
meaning of her remark, Doc Feathers said, "Lawney, I can use you," and she moved away.

Bevins said, his voice meant for Rhianon alone,
"She was brought up in a different world."

"And you?" Rhianon asked.

Bevins put a hand on Rhianon's shoulder. "I
went through a long and bloody war. But until I
came to Arizona, I thought the killing was over."

Somebody lifted the lantern, and its glow spread
and erased part of the night. Doc Feathers
mumbled something, in a tone incredulous and angry. There was a sound of tearing cloth. Lawney
Bevens voiced a stifled "Oh!" and the lantern
swayed wildly, making shadows that expanded and
diminished grotesquely in this small world of orange glow.

Rhianon turned to see Doc Feathers come to his
feet and take the lantern from Lawney Bevins. He
was a rounded man with a huge, reddish-gray

moustache that turned fiercely upward at the ends. He wore a black frock coat that was too small to pull together and button; and a straw skimmer, like the ones Rhianon had seen pictures of in the eastern papers, seemed to be held up by his ears.

He said, "Your friend?"

"Yes," Rhianon answered.

"Badly busted up, both inside as well as outside. It will take a while."

"I can wait a while," Rhianon said.

VI

RHIANON AWAKENED that next morning with the guilty feeling of a man who has slept through part of the morning's work. He opened one eye, stared up at the wagon's brake beam, felt a moment of brief panic until he gathered his wits enough to remember where he was and how he got there, then crawled out from his soogans.

The smell of fresh coffee wafted to him as he tugged at his bootstraps. There was a general bustle that bespoke of a busy community at work. He rolled up his soogans, crawled toward the Conestoga's rear axle, brushed his shoulders against the wagon jack and the tar bucket, and came into the open.

Prairie and farm wagons, most of them covered with canvas or homespun, dotted the landscape. A few tents squatted among them, and cooking fires still crackled in the still morning air. A woman's voice lifted in an old, old song as she hung clothing on a line stretched from a brake lever to a mesquite bush; a hatless man in bib overalls was hammering a brace onto the moldboard of a plow.

A tow-headed boy of nine or ten jumped from

behind a water barrel, pointed a finger at Rhianon, and shouted, "Bang!"

Rhianon said gravely, "All right, I'm dead."

"You're supposed to lie down," the boy said. "You want to die with your boots off, don't you?"

"Most of all," Rhianon answered, "I want some breakfast."

"You're going the wrong way. Miss Lawney's over yonder cooking something now. Have you killed any Indians with that gun?"

"Not lately," Rhianon said, and he pointed his finger at the boy, cocked his thumb back and then suddenly dropped his hand to his side. He made his way past the Conestoga's near side, stepped over the angled tongue, and came upon Lawney Bevins. She was kneeling under a tent fly propped up with dried mescal stalks, stirring something in a pot.

Rhianon said, "Morning," and touched his hat brim.

Lawney Bevins turned and made a small gesture with her chin. "Wash up over there, Mr. Rhianon. Coffee's ready, and there will be supawn in a minute."

Rhianon said, "Yes, ma'am," and couldn't hide the faint doubtful tone in his voice.

"Cornmeal mush," Lawney said tartly, and turned her attention again to the pot.

Rhianon stepped over to the upended barrel that served as a commode, poured water into a sand-scratched porcelain bowl, and obediently washed up, remembering not to snort.

When he finished, he used the soapy water to shave himself, using the straight razor Colonel Bevins had left there for him. By the time he finished this chore and slicked his black hair back he was thoroughly awake and ravenously hungry. To his vast surprise, the mush was excellent, golden brown and laced with bacon rinds. He ate two helpings of it, washing it down with scalding coffee, before he ventured to bring up the subject uppermost in his mind.

"How is he?"

Lawney Bevins, turning away from the dishpan, said, "The same. I wondered when you would ask. The doctor looked in on him this morning, early." She studied him with a long and close regard, her eyes, turned the deepest blue in this morning light, frankly scanning him.

"Awake?" he asked.

"For a few minutes," she answered. "Doctor said all we can give him is rest and hope."

"That would cure the sickness of half the world," he said, and came to his feet. "All right to look in on him?"

"Be quiet," she answered. "He's in the wagon."

He stacked his dishes and cup, and placed them on the rough boards she was using as a work table, then walked back to the rear of the wagon. Looking over the tailgate, he could see Miles Brandes stretched out there, a red and blue checked comforter thrown over him. Brandes was asleep, but breathing heavily. A white bandage covered the upper part of his head. One side of his face from temple to jawline was scraped almost entirely bare of skin; some sort of salve spread upon it made it look like wet beefsteak.

Rhianon said softly, "Miles—Miles!" and shook his head.

Lawney Bevins, coming up behind him, said, "He must be a very good friend."

"We were kids together. We were planning to be partners."

"In a business?"

"Selling horses." His voice quickened. "You've seen the mustangs in this part of the country. They're wiry and fast and good for some chores, but people want bigger horses with more strength and bottom. Especially the army." He found himself talking more than he intended, and he gave her a doubtful look. "You're not really interested in this?"

"I didn't even know you could talk. Have another cup of coffee and tell me more."

Seated on an upended tomato crate, Rhianon let his coffee grow cold as he found himself unaccountably pouring out all his hopes and plans for the future, wondering all the while what there was about the girl that could draw him out so. It was years since he had talked to anybody in this way. He had meant to limit this to a few terse remarks, but now that he was started he found he couldn't stop.

He said eventually, "Well, that's about it. You buy horses in California, drive them across to Arizona, and sell at a good profit. Good living for a man."

She was seated on the ground in front of him, crosslegged like a child, her hands resting in her lap.

"You mentioned a brother," she said. "What happened to him?"

A shadow fell across his face, darkening his eyes. He looked at her without answering, this shadow still lying over him and erasing all the brave dreams that had lent his countenance a vital brightness as he talked.

"You've said more than you think," Lawney Bevins said softly. "And the fears you haven't uttered are as darkly clear as the bright dreams you voiced."

"Mighty fancy talk," he said.

"I read books as well as people. In both, you learn to place together the things that haven't been said." She lifted her hands from her lap and turned them palms up in a small and swift gesture. "Shall I put some of your pieces together?"

He came slowly to his feet, feeling vaguely uncomfortable as though he had opened his clothing to reveal old scars that even he had refused to look at. He felt himself a fool for talking so much. This was a thing he had never before let himself do; for it was a part of his calling to let others look upon him as a cold, implacable machine and never see beyond the star that once he wore so brightly.

He wanted to say, "No," but something more than curiosity swept over him and had its way with him. He put the empty coffee cup down, staring over the valley's flat reaches, feeling the intense and steady strike of her gaze upon him. Her voice lifted to him as though from a far distance.

"You saw the emptiness of your own life. But your younger brother saw only the way the other men looked up to you and envied you because of the way you wore your star and the way it shone in the flash of your guns. For a time he lived in your shadow. Then he broke away to make his own shadow."

Rhianon said, "It was darker than he thought."

She went on as though he had not spoken. "But you were too busy keeping your star bright to go after him and stop him before it was too late. Then something made you quit—and you and your friend set about to make the dream you'd once had come true. You thought to make your brother a part of it, but you knew he wouldn't talk to you. So your friend offered to contact him and he found your brother here in Coffin Rock. Then he wrote you to come. You did—and now—now he'll never drive horses across the Colorado."

"He will," Rhianon said fiercely. "He's got to!"

She arose lithely, brushed off her skirts, and laid a hand on his arm. "I'm sorry. It was a poor way to tell you."

He looked quickly down at her. "The doctor say that?"

She nodded. "He has a chance to live. That is something to hope for. But Doctor Feathers said no more riding, no matter how well he may heal up."

"It was his whole life," Rhianon said. "Raising horses, breaking horses. What good is it for him to live? He'll die again every time he looks at a saddle."

She said in a voice scarcely more than a murmur, "What would he want you to do?"

He slanted a long look down upon her, prolonged and thoughtful. "You're right. I can give him that much."

"Your brother, too," she said. She stepped back from him. "I've been listening again to words you never said, but it's my guess he's with Qualtrough and Colvig."

"Not any more," he said, and turned away to find his horse.

Third Wellington sighed heavily, gave some consideration to tilting his chair back, and for about the fortieth time thought better of this notion. The last time he had tried it, the two rear legs of the chair had snapped off like toothpicks, and the cost of repair came out of his own pocket. He brought his feet carefully down from the desk top and eyed the bunk with a speculative and longing interest. But he knew he would fall immediately asleep there, and with two prisoners in the cells that was something he couldn't afford to do.

Since he couldn't sit comfortably and didn't dare lie down, there was nothing else to do but get to his feet. He stood beside the desk a moment, yawning hugely, adjusted the lamp wick, then walked back toward the cells.

There were three cells, each just large enough for a bunk and a small table. The center one had long ago been converted into a sort of catchall for the accumulation of all those things not good enough to use but too good to throw away. Wellington swore every morning that he would get to cleaning it out that very day, but somehow he never seemed to be able to get around to it.

Wellington hung the lamp on a bent nail, hitched up his sagging trousers, cuffed his derby back, and peered into the cells. Linus Pauncefoote was stretched out on the bunk of the cell to the right. His gusty snores slid through the bars. Wellington listened a moment, wondering how a man's meanness could even come through in his snoring, then walked over to the other cell.

He said in a low voice, "Asleep?"

The huddled form on the bunk moved restlessly.

"Sure. I always sleep good on a nail mattress. Why don't you just leave me the hell alone?"

"Just checking," Wellington said mildly. "Head all right?"

"Rub it in," Johnny Minstrel said bitterly. "My time will come tomorrow. You know that, don't you? Qualtrough will have me out of here so fast you won't see nothing but dust. No damn reason me being here, anyway."

Some truth to that last statement, Wellington mused. Pauncefoote, yes. But the kid hadn't done a thing, no matter what his first intentions might have been. It was pretty evident that Colvig had set the kid up to make a play against Rhianon, all right. That much was plain as a Mexican brand. The rest of it, though, was mighty unclear. Rhianon simply backed the kid against the saloon wall, then bent a gun barrel over his head. You could tell the kid had wanted to make a play, but something held him back until that last split-second when it was too late. Not that he looked scared, either. It was something else.

Johnny Minstrel raised himself on one elbow and said, "You just going to stand there and gawk and let that damn light shine in my eyes?"

"Feels like we might get some rain in a day or two." Wellington said thoughtfully. He lifted the lamp from the nail and ambled back into his office.

At his desk again, he busied himself shuffling through the assorted papers that had accumulated during the past month, ending up by throwing all of them into the trash box. Not much point in bothering with them, anyhow—he would sure as hell be out of a job soon after Qualtrough got back tomorrow.

His thoughts veered then to Rhianon, and he wondered why the man had thrown away his star and what he was doing in Coffin Rock. And especially what made Johnny Minstrel so important to him. Normally, in this country you buffalo a man and then you just let him lay. But Rhianon had insisted the kid be jailed and held until he returned to talk to him. Besides all this, there was something more than plain human sympathy in Rhianon's feeling for that drifter who Pauncefoote dragged.

This whole damned day, Wellington thought morosely, was beset with mysteries. Not the least of which was his own about-face. He'd been marshal of Coffin Rock since before it even had a name. Not much of a job, but there wasn't much work to it, either. Then Qualtrough showed up, started making the town boom and promised a railroad coming through. And all Third Wellington had to do was lick a couple boots now and then, shut his eyes at the proper time, and he would end up as a bigtown lawman with twice the pay.

Then this Rhianon had to show up and make a man take a good hard look at himself.

Wellington stood up, sucked in his belly, and raked his derby down over one eye. A smoky gray light filtered through the oil-papered east window; the roosters over at Mama Pellingrino's chicken farm set up a ridiculous tumult; somebody over toward the Shoo-Fly banged a trash can.

Wellington grubbed in the desk drawer for a

cigar, swiped a match across the crown of his derby, and lit up. He threw the door open and stared out at the Coffin's dismal bulk, letting each exhalation of smoke out slowly as though each puff might be the last.

It was going to be a hell of a day.

The sun was high over the Peloncillos by the time Rhianon hit the outskirts of Coffin Rock. The day had already gathered enough heat to drive him out of his coat; he folded it and tied it behind the cantle. Sweat beaded his forehead and dampened his hatband. The edge of a dark cloud showed over Hell's Rim; the faint drum of distant thunder rolled upon the air. He reined the black past the Coffin's westerly side, and pulled up in front of the jail.

Third Wellington threw the door open before he could knock, saying in a resigned tone, "Come on in. Damn shame every day has to start with a morning."

Rhianon said, "Prisoners had breakfast?"

"Just thinking to take them over to the Shoo-Fly. Serve them right."

"Take Pauncefoote. I want to talk to the kid."

"Plumb irregular," Wellington complained. "But what hasn't been these days?" He hitched his gunbelt up higher across his paunch and went to the cells, coming back presently with Pauncefoote.

Pauncefoote threw Rhianon a wicked look on the way out, saying, "You're both dead. You damn well better know that."

Third Wellington laid a beefy hand on the man's back and propelled him through the door. He said darkly, "Shoo-Fly will get us all first, anyway. Sashay, sonny," and slammed the door behind him.

Rhianon walked back to Johnny Minstrel's cell. Johnny, tucking in his shirttail, gave him an icy look through the bars and deliberately turned his back.

"All right, boy," Rhianon said, "this was the only way I could make you stand still long enough to talk to you."

"Do your augering somewheres else," Johnny Minstrel said. "I heard enough of it for near twenty years."

"You're making me do this the hard way," Rhianon said in a level voice. "You want out of here or not?"

"I'll get out, anyway. When Qualtrough gets back. One way or another. Just be sure you ain't in the way when it happens."

"All right." Rhianon sighed. "When you're ready to listen to some sense, let Wellington know. You'll stay in that cell until you do."

"Will I now?" Johnny Minstrel said. He turned to face his brother, and his eyes glistened with a wintry hatred. "Will I bygod now?"

VII

THIRD WELLINGTON snapped the handcuffs
back upon Linus Pauncefoote, picked up the skillet
of ham and eggs, and prodded Pauncefoote out the
Shoo-Fly's sagging door. They barely passed
beyond the shade of the wooden awning when Wellington saw Josh Spurlock and two other men cut
across from the Coffin's morning shadows and
plant themselves solidly across the board walk. *I
don't have enough troubles,* he thought irritably.
*Now I got to face a committee of right-thinking citi-
zens.* He let out a gusty breath, speeded
Pauncefoote's lagging steps with a prod of the gun
muzzle where it would do the most good, and came
to a halt only when Spurlock hailed him.

"Wellington—think we better have a little talk."

"Ham and eggs getting cold," Wellington said.
"Hungry man waiting for them." He recognized
the other two now—Cap Horner, the barber, and
Duff Walker, who owned the Acme Assay Company. He added then, "You boys look serious
enough for a baptizing. Pauncefoote, stop skittering or I'll blast your pants off!"

Josh Spurlock edged forward, thumbs caught

under the lapels of his striped coat. "Wellington, as mayor of Coffin Rock, and with the backing of the city council, we're a kind of committee to make a formal demand.

"Sounds important," Wellington said gravely. "I never had a formal demand made of me before."

Spurlock gave him an anxious look, licked his upper lip, then apparently decided to plunge in. "We want you to let them two prisoners go."

Wellington said, "Reckon not, boys." He threw a quick look at Pauncefoote, gripped the shotgun with his elbow, then removed his derby and placed it over the skillet. "Eggs lose heat fast," he said.

Cap Horner pushed past Spurlock. "Wellington, look. This is just plain common sense. Colvig is just hanging onto Qualtrough's shirttail. Qualtrough goes away for a couple days, and Colvig lets two of his men get jailed. How do you think that will set with Qualtrough?"

"Like locoweed in a cow's belly," Wellington said cheerfully.

"So," Horner pressed on, "you know what Colvig's got to do. Qualtrough will be back on the three o'clock stage. Colvig has got to get those men out before then, or he loses his job and his easy money. Qualtrough can find somebody else to take his place."

"No skin off my nose," Wellington said.

"You miss the point," Spurlock snapped. "If them prisoners ain't let out, Colvig will have to take them out." His voice took on a righteous tone. "Our community has had more than enough violence since that killer, Rhianon, came butting into our affairs."

"Oh, brother," Wellington murmured. "It's a wonder even Pauncefoote here can stand that."

"With a shotgun looking up my tail I can stand anything," Pauncefoote grumbled.

Duff Walker said, "This can be done real easy and no harm to anybody. Just ride out of town a piece and leave your keys on the desk."

"And take your friend, Rhianon, with you," Spurlock added. "After all, this is an order from your mayor and the city council."

"Mr. Spurlock," Wellington said softly, "have you ever read the territorial laws regarding the duties and responsibilities of a village marshal? If you haven't, I've got a copy I just dusted off."

"Damned if I understand your attitude anymore," Spurlock blurted out.

"Hardly do myself," Wellington said. "Been walking around on my knees so long I forgot what my feet were for. Gents, the ham and eggs are getting cold, and my head is frying. Pauncefoote, start putting one leg in front of the other."

Balancing the derby-topped skillet carefully, Wellington prodded Pauncefoote past the three men, ignoring their outraged stares. He was more surprised at himself than he cared to admit, and he wondered now if he had made the right decision. Spurlock and the others might have made their request from a wrong motive, but they were nevertheless right. Colvig would have to make a play to release Pauncefoote and Minstrel, and he would have to do it before Qualtrough returned. That would be the only way he could prove to Qualtrough he could still handle things.

He threw a look at the sun, and caught another

glimpse of the clouds forming along the edge of Hell's Rim. A gust of wind sent a newspaper skittering along the street, and a sound of far-off thunder swept along in its wake. Time for the summer rains. Coffin Rock was getting mighty hot. Ever since this Rhianon arrived Coffin Rock was getting mighty hot.

Rhianon waited silently while Third Wellington locked Pauncefoote in his cell and served the ham and eggs to Johnny. Rhianon had looked out upon the street and seen Wellington talking to Spurlock and the other two men, and had some idea of what must have been said. He waited until Wellington came back into the office before voicing his thoughts.

"Want to release them?"

"Yup," Wellington grunted. He carefully examined his derby, sniffed dubiously at the sweatband, then plopped it on his head. "No harm done. Just a little grease. The good citizens think Colvig will try to break the boys out lessen we let them out aforehand."

"What do you think?"

"Guess he'll have to try," Wellington answered glumly. "He's already made one mistake. Qualtrough has got people here buffaloed into the idea that nobody can go against him. Now two of his gunslingers are in jail. That's going to start everybody thinking. Colvig ain't much on brains, but he knows he's got to right this mistake on his own before Qualtrough gets back."

Rhianon lifted his head suddenly and strode to the window. "Couple riders," he said quietly. "The one with the beard and the one-eyed joker."

"Hank Parsons and Patch Vermillion," Wellington said. "Well, that makes it sure."

Rhianon said, "Your town, Wellington. Which way do you aim to play it?"

"Never cared much for trouble," Wellington said. "But a thought just come to me. No doubt about Pauncefoote deserving jail. But it's a mite hard to find anything to charge the kid with. Maybe we can work a deal—"

"The kid stays," Rhianon said sharply.

"Man can try," Wellington said in a resigned voice. "Just one favor. Since we're going to spend the next two-three hours bleeding over each other, I'd like to know why."

"He's my brother," Rhianon said softly. "That answer it?"

"Ah," Wellington sighed. "That answers it. Part of it, anyway—but it's enough." His button-round eyes regarded Rhianon with a new interest. "What is it you want?"

"I want to take my brother away from here. I want Pauncefoote held for trial."

"Man die?"

"Not yet," Rhianon murmured. "And if he lives he'll be a cripple the rest of his life."

"All right. You tell me what you want me to do."

"Don't want a fight unless we have to," Rhianon said. "There a back way out of here?"

"Door over by the side of Pauncefoote's cell, but it won't do us any good. Used to be an old Spanish mission behind the jail. Nothing standing now except a wall. Runs clear along from the corner of the Coffin Saloon almost up to the Shoo-Fly. All of ten foot high. Man standing at either end can box us in. Likely that's where Vermillion and Parsons are now."

"We'll just have a look," Rhianon said, and stepped quickly to the jail's rear section. Linus Pauncefoote, indolently smoking a cigarette, pointed a sardonic finger at him as he passed by the cell, and said, "Bang!" and his mocking laughter followed Rhianon to the rear door.

Rhianon, grunting, lifted the heavy bar away and stepped outside into the alley made by the adobe wall. He threw a quick look to his left and saw a man sitting in a half-slumped position on a horse. He turned his gaze to the other end of the alley and at first saw nothing. Then a man stepped quietly from a building's angle and touched his hat in an ironic salute.

Passing back into the office, he went immediately to the gun rack, selected a Winchester .73, checked the magazine tube, and levered a cartridge into the chamber.

Wellington said, "They there?"

Rhianon nodded, then opened the front door and stepped to the plank walk. The Coffin hid his view of the street's other side, but the street on this side of the big rock was clear, and he could see no dust on the road leading toward town.

He went back inside, saying, "Just those two so far. They're watching the back. Why not anybody in front?"

"There will be," Wellington brooded. "We don't have horses, anyway. All they got to do is wait." He stomped over to the desk, scooped a cigar from the drawer, and lit up. "Just an idle thought, maybe, but supposing things get rough—which side will your brother take?"

"I don't know," Rhianon said honestly.

"If you get him out of here," Wellington said, "I hope you take him over your knee and tan his bottom."

Rhianon pulled his old Horologe from a vest pocket and glanced at it. It was nearly noon. A growing murmur of voices broke against the door; boots stirred the street's dust, and a man's angry voice said, "Dammit, shut up! I'll do the talking!"

"Spurlock," Wellington said. "Colvig's going to let the good citizens have another try."

The murmur subsided, then swelled. A steady tramping reverberated along the plank walk. A man's head briefly appeared at the front window, and was as swiftly withdrawn. Josh Spurlock's insistent voice called out, "Wellington!"

"I'm suddenly a popular man." Wellington sighed, and came to his feet.

Rhianon said quickly, "I brought this on. Let me talk to them."

Wellington said doubtfully, "Seems to me I'm the one wearing the badge."

There was something in Wellington's voice that made Rhianon look at the fat lawman more closely. Understanding came to him. He said, "So used to wearing a star I forgot I wasn't anymore. You play the hand, Wellington."

"Always wanted to say a few well-chosen words to Spurlock," Wellington drawled. He dropped the cigar into the cuspidor, settled his derby firmly down upon his ears, picked up the shotgun, and stepped outside. He squarely faced the group of fifteen or twenty men who were ranged in an irregular mass in front of the jail. Josh Spurlock stood in front, his mouth drawn into a tight line.

Wellington waited quietly, letting them have their look. He said then, "Now, boys, don't make no fool play."

Spurlock said, his sideburns quivering, "You going to let those men go?"

Somebody in the rear called out, "Hell, go in and take them! That fat tinstar can't stop us!"

Wellington swung the shotgun, loosely covering Spurlock. "Fine bunch of honest citizens you've gathered here, Mr. Mayor. That forty-rod the Bull-dog sells must be a real brave-maker."

Spurlock flushed. He said, doggedly persistent, "We asked you real nice once. Wellington, what makes you so damned stubborn anyway? You been eating raw meat?"

Wellington said in a deceptively level voice, "The purpose of this little gathering, I reckon, is to persuade me peaceful-like to let those two men go free so Colvig won't start shooting holes in my jail."

Bob Horner pushed his way forward, saying, "We'll be honest about this. If Colvig starts something, we'll all have to join with him. We all know what will happen to us if we don't."

Wellington said, "Bob, you see that man get dragged?"

"Don't make any difference," Horner said doggedly. "We all—"

"You see him?" Wellington asked again.

"Well, yes," Horner muttered.

"You think the man who done it shouldn't stand trial?"

Josh Spurlock said curtly, "Now look here, Wellington. Once in a while concessions have to be made. Damn it, man, once in a while you have to think of the community as a whole."

"I've been thinking of it," Wellington drawled. "Pretty sorry lot, ain't we? We had a pretty nice little town here. Then somebody comes in with a little money and a lot of promises and we all sell our souls. I didn't realize what a butt-kisser I'd become until a real man came to town and made me look at myself. All right, I'll make you a proposition. Here's a chance for all of you to get up off your knees and feel like men again. We make up a posse and escort these two prisoners to Willcox."

A stunned silence fell over the group of men. Somebody drew wind with a prolonged "Aaaah!" Bob Horner threw his arms out in a hopeless gesture, and Spurlock's frown deepened.

"Well?" Wellington pursued.

Horner said, "My God, how far do you think Colvig and his bunch would let us get?"

"Seven or eight of them. Twenty of you," Wellington said calmly.

"We're not professional gunslingers," Spurlock protested.

"Fifteen minutes to make your minds up," Wellington said.

VIII

WATCHING WELLINGTON close the door against the protesting voice, Rhianon was glad he had let the fat lawman talk to the crowd. There was a decisive spring to Wellington's stride that hadn't been there before; his eyes burned with a brighter light. He said, "Wild Bill Hickok couldn't have put it to them any straighter. You know these people. What do you think?

Wellington leaned the shotgun against the desk, yanked out his bandanna and wiped sweat from his forehead. "Couldn't have done it without knowing you was in here backing me up. Don't know what they'll decide. Got some of them thinking, but it will take more than a few words. They ain't bad people, Rhianon. It's just that they've been rotting here in this godforsaken hole in the middle of no-where for too long a time. Then suddenly Qualtrough appears and gives them all a look at the land of milk and honey, and now they're scared it's going to be taken away from them."

"Not realizing," Rhianon observed, "that they'll end up with nothing but the skim and the comb anyway." He shook his head. "This town. You wonder what it's doing here."

"Halfway to somewhere," Wellington said. "That's the story of every town from Westport to San Francisco. Everyplace is halfway to somewheres else."

"Any truth to this railroad story?"

"Some," Wellington said. "Railroad is coming through the valley, all right. And unless things change somewhat, it'll go through Coffin Rock. Mainly just because there's a town already here. Qualtrough has promised a station, loading pens, and Lord knows what all to the railroad people. Colonel Bevins and his settlement have made a try to get the rails through their area. Little more in a direct line, but there's nothing there. Settlement can't even get lumber for building."

Rhianon said, "Odd. Seems to be plenty available in Coffin Rock."

"Army taking all they can mill in the Peloncillos. Have to go west into the Chiricahuas. Qualtrough's wagons somehow get through. The settlement's don't."

Rhianon frowned. He took another look at his Horologe. "Another five minutes. About those wagons not getting through. Why aren't they?"

"Apaches," Wellington said.

"Uh-uh. Geronimo is in Mexico. Loco was leading a small band of raiders awhile, but they've all been rounded up. Might be a few braves skulking around, hoping to pick up a scalp, but there's no band large enough to raid a wagon train."

"Maybe not," Wellington said. "But Indians or no Indians, somebody's been hitting those supply trains the settlement folks send out. All I know is what I hear. When you get a chance, you might talk to Bevins about what you think. Providing," he added wryly, "you're going to be able to talk to anybody."

"About time," Rhianon murmured. He threw the door open and called, "Spurlock! Made up your mind?" He made a tall and easy target in the sun's slanting wash, but this was the only way he knew how to play it. There was no answer. He thought: *Still talking it over,* and was starting to move back inside when the shot rolled across from the Coffin and chunked into the wall beside him, scattering flakes of adobe.

He caught the glint of a rifle barrel, quickly withdrawn, at the top of the Coffin. He stepped swiftly back into the jail's interior, latched the door and threw the cross-bar across it.

Rhino Colvig's voice called out, "That was just to show you we ain't fooling, Rhianon. Your sandy didn't work. Send those two men out, and you and Fatty can ride out of town."

Wellington snorted and sucked in his gut.

Rhianon moved to the window, caught the shutter with the front sight of his Winchester and pulled it to. There wasn't any point in answering. Colvig knew the game and the chances as well as he. The pattern had been laid down before either man was born, and they would have to follow its deadly rules, each side knowing what the other's next move would be, and neither being able to deviate a hairbreadth to change the handwriting already etched in gunsmoke.

Rhianon motioned to Wellington to move against the wall. Scattered shots came from across the street, thunking into the adobe and kicking sharp splinters out of the boards of the door and window shutter. He knew what the strategy would be—drive them back where their firing area would be restricted, then ram the door under cover of fire. They'd try to knock that window shutter out first, perhaps, and he knew it wouldn't hold out much longer.

He leanred back against the adobe that spaced the door and window, thankful that some old settler had built these walls two feet thick. Gunfire rolled in a steady thunder, setting up an odd thrumming in his ears. They had figured out the window business by now, and more splinters were appearing.

Third Wellington moved restively, and said, "Mite warm hereabouts."

"It will be warmer," Rhianon promised, and ducked a flying splinter from the window shutter. He was wondering what he could do about that window when the gunfire ceased as suddenly and shockingly as it began.

He waited a long breathless moment, not knowing what to make of this. He threw Wellington a look, and murmured, "Now that is an odd thing," and inched cautiously to the window. He peered carefully through a rip in the shutter, and at first could see nothing. Then through the dust and smoke he caught a dim and dust-hazed glimpse of somebody crossing the street toward the jail. In another moment he was afforded a full, clear look, and drew in a sharp breath.

Wellington said fretfully, "What the hell's going on?"

Rhianon, not answering, was at the door by the time Wellington's question died in the still air. He lifted out the cross-bar and set it aside, then listened carefully, waiting until he heard heels strike the plank walk. He threw the door open, saying in a softly wondering way, "Come in, Lawney."

Wellington gave a low whistle, swept his derby back, and scratched his head.

Lawney Bevins waited until Rhianon barred the door behind her, then said in a voice so low Rhianon could hardly hear it, "You're not hurt—either of you?"

Rhianon shook his head. Words formed in his mind and lost themselves in the devious trails of his thoughts.

Lawney Bevins said, "They gave me five minutes. I told them I thought I could persuade you to give your prisoners up."

"Did you now?" Rhianon said with a faint, distant civility. He had thought she knew him better than this, and he could not altogether mask his hurt.

She said in a reluctant voice, "I take it the answer is no."

Rhianon nodded his head stiffly. "Miss Bevins, this is the second time you've done this. If I were your pappy I'd take you over my knees and—"

"You aren't," she cut in. "And I knew just what you were going to say. All right, Mr. Rhianon—how can I help?" She moved to the desk chair and sat down, her hands folded primly on her lap.

"If we could find a way to get out through the alley," Rhianon mused. "Wellington, was the whole bunch in yesterday?"

"All I've ever seen," Wellington answered.

"Six of them," Rhianon said. "And Pauncefoote made seven. We've got two of them here, and Colvig has a man stationed at each end of the alley. That leaves only three on the rock. Miss Bevins, any of the town people in on this?"

She shook her head. "A few of them looking on. They'll stand aside and watch you be slaughtered, but they'll take no active part in it."

"How did you get into town?"

"The spring wagon."

Rhianon raised his head sharply, and said, "Ah!"

"Whatever you're planning," Wellington said glumly, "I ain't going to like it."

"Buildings solid from the Shoo-Fly to the Coffin Saloon," Rhianon said. "Which is the length of the wall. Can a wagon pass down the alley without being seen from the top of the Coffin?"

"If you hug close to the rear of the buildings," Wellington answered. "Climbed up once to have a look. I see what you're getting at, but the trouble is, Colvig has a man guarding each end of the alley."

"Won't be for long," said Rhianon. "What do you figure Colvig's next move will be?"

"Ram the door," Wellington said promptly.

"Keno," said Rhianon. "And that will take three men. They'll need at least two men shooting from the rock to cover them. That means Colvig will have to draw off the two jokers covering the alley. He'll feel safe doing that now because he knows we don't have horses and couldn't get far, even if we left the prisoners behind."

Lawney Bevins asked calmly, "What do you want me to do?"

"Go back, tell them we said for them to come and get us. Get into your wagon and start up the road as though you were going back to the settlement. They won't try to stop you because they know it would take you two-three hours to get there and bring back help. By that time, it would be too late. As soon as you reach a point where you can't be seen, circle back and come up behind the Shoo-Fly. Leave the wagon there."

Rhianon gave Lawney Bevins a doubtful look. "I don't know what to tell you from here on. Just one thing. Where are their horses?"

"Other side of the Coffin," she said quickly, and came to her feet. "I'll see what I can do. The wagon will be there."

A single shot rang out, and when its echoes died away a voice shouted, "Long enough! Send her back out!"

Lawney Bevins moved toward the door, walking slowly and letting her fingers trail over the desk. Some deep feeling that Rhianon couldn't define welled up in her eyes; she put her hand on the door latch, then turned swiftly to Rhianon and said, "Good luck," and was gone.

Rhianon watched her through the window until she arrived near the Coffin's base at the street's other side. Rhino Colvig came to meet her, listened intently to something she was saying, then turned away, one arm heavily slicing the air.

Rhianon moved back into the jail office, meeting Wellington's inquisitive stare.

Wellington said, "For a peace-loving woman,

she sure turns up in the dangedest places. Rhianon, how do we work this?"

"Help me with this," Rhianon said, and together they dragged the heavy desk over to the door. "It won't stop them, but it will give us a few extra seconds in case we need them." He took a look through the broken shutter. A rider dragging a large cottonwood log halted at the Coffin's base. Two men moved up and shifted the log, and the rider coiled his rope and spurred away. A shot whined into the window frame, and Rhianon withdrew his head swiftly.

Wellington said, "We likely can make this on our own. But are you forgetting we got a couple ornery prisoners to reckon with?"

"They'll sleep through it," Rhianon said.

"Ah," Wellington sighed. He started back to the cells. "No time like the present."

"Take the kid," Rhianon said. "I'll have more pleasure with Pauncefoote."

Pauncefoote merely raised an eyebrow as Rhianon and Wellington entered the cell block; but the planes of Johnny Minstrel's face became awash with alarm, and his eyes turned dollar-round.

"What's this?" he asked as Wellington unlocked the door.

"Bedtime," Wellington said. "Turn around."

Rhianon and Wellington dragged the two unconscious men to the rear door, bound feet and hands and gagged them with two of Wellington's faded bandannas.

Rhianon said, "About ten minutes. Think she's had time?"

"Doubt it," Wellington answered. He was panting heavily and held on to one of the cell bars as he came to his feet. "Have to go a pretty good piece down the road before you get out of sight of a man on top of the rock."

"We'll delay them a little," Rhianon said, and made for the office. There was no way to take aim without getting his head blown off, but he stood back from the window and triggered a group of shots through the splintered shutter.

An answering fusillade came from across the street, lead whining through the room and ricocheting wickedly against the adobe walls.

Wellington crouched behind the desk, making himself as small as possible. "What's all this for? We can't see to hit anything, anyway."

"Got to keep letting them know we're here. Stop shooting, and they might think to send a man down to check the alley. Those last shots came from only one angle. That means they've pulled only one man away. We wait until they start hitting us from both sides. Then we make our play."

"Interesting," Wellington drawled. "Just what the hell play are you talking about?"

Rhianon levered a cartridge into the chamber, triggered another shot through the window. "I head down the alley for the wagon. You stay here, throw a couple rounds once in a while to let them think we're both here. Use both the rifle and the shotgun. I'll bring the wagon down, we load the boys into it, and light a shuck."

"Have to turn off behind the Coffin Saloon," Wellington said. "Rough country and no road. And they'll be riding after us in less than five minutes."

"Not if I've judged that girl right," Rhianon said.

"No man can judge any woman right," Wellington grumbled.

A shot spanged through the shutter, sending a splinter flying across the room. Close upon it came another, angling from the other side.

"Both up there now," Rhianon said. "Time for me to make my break." He moved away from the wall, tossed the Winchester to Wellington. "Keep them busy."

"Sounds like dandy fun," Wellington growled. He came to one knee to fire, ducking instantly back when a shot roared through the window and shaved a corner of the desk.

Rhianon ran to the rear, stepped over the limp bodies of Pauncefoote and Johnny Minstrel, and opened the door cautiously. He held his breath, half-expecting a shot, but none came. He waited a long moment, hearing the dull boom of Wellington's shotgun answered by rifle fire.

"Only one way to really tell," he murmured, and stepped into the alley. Tension gripped him and made his shoulder muscles ache, but he took his full look at both ends of the alley.

"Clear so far," he told himself. He ran in a low crouch toward the Shoo-Fly.

There was a bad moment when he came to Horner's old barber shop, for there was an open space a couple feet wide. This held him while he considered the chances. Then he walked slowly past, reckoning Colvig and his bunch would be too busy concentrating on the jail to notice his passing. He only hoped the same would be true when he brought the wagon by here.

He came to the rear of the Shoo-Fly digging deep for wind, and immediately cast about for the wagon. As he looked, the firing swelled to a steady roar. They would be moving up to ram the door soon.

The wall petered out here, ending in a sloping rubble of fallen adobe bricks. He cut straight across to this, taking his chances of being seen from the Elephant Corral, thinking Lawney Bevins could have brought the wagon up behind this end of the wall.

Rounding the pile of adobe, he had his look.

IX

His FIRST FEELING of bitter disappointment changed to one of relief. For the thought of the danger Lawney Bevins was exposing herself to was a nagging worry that had never left him. He hoped the answer was that she hadn't been able to find a place to turn off without being seen, and immediately turned his thoughts to this moment's problem. He couldn't leave Wellington alone to face Colvig's attack. The two of them might still escape, but there would be no way to take the prisoners with them.

He was still caught in this grim moment of indecision when he heard a sound that instantly turned him. He palmed into leather as Lawney Bevins, from the seat of the spring wagon, said, "I had to go farther than I thought."

Her hair was disheveled and a long rip in one sleeve revealed a roundly firm arm; but her voice was calm and she held the reins steadily.

Rhianon stepped to the side of the wagon and said, "Get down."

She gave him a sharpened look. "No. I'm coming with you."

"Not this way," he said, and held a hand up to her. "Don't want you there in case they break through before we can get started. Run along the outside of the wall. We'll pick you up when we turn out by the other end."

She was hesitant, but she could see this made sense, and she let him help her down.

"Better get started," he said, and vaulted into the seat.

This first part of it, bringing the wagon from the wall's end into the alley behind the buildings, would be the most dangerous. Then there was that open space beside the barber shop. He could only hope that the men on the rock would be busy enough concentrating on the jail that they wouldn't see the wagon. He wrapped the reins around his hand, said "Haw!" and turned the wagon into the alley.

Time seemed to stop and turn in upon itself. This trip of less than a hundred yards seemed interminable. He hugged the building walls, scraping the side of the wagon against them, waiting for the spang of a rifle bullet and a yell that he was seen. The tension was so strong in him, blanketing all his other senses, that he would have overshot the jail if Third Wellington hadn't stepped out and grabbed the bridle.

"Couple passengers to pick up," Wellington rumbled. "High time, too. Think they're fixing to ram the door."

Rhianon leapt down from the seat, found an adobe brick to anchor the reins, and raced to the door to help Wellington drag the prisoners out. The gunfire was making the horses spooky;

Rhianon twice had to use his weight on their cheek
straps before he and Wellington managed to lift the
two bound men over the tailgate into the wagon.
Wellington clambered over into the wagon bed
with the prisoners, while Rhianon took the reins
and crouched down between the dash and the
seat.

This last run was easier, for the adobe buildings
formed a solid barrier. The alleyway between the
wall and buildings was hardpan. There was no fear
of raising a dust, and Rhianon drove the horses at
full gallop, knowing the steady gunfire would muf-
fle this hoof thunder. The wall at this end had cor-
nered, cutting off sharply and cleanly, and
Rhianon swept the wagon around it, reining in behind.

Lawney Bevins came from the corner's angle,
gave her hand, and was lifted into the seat beside
Rhianon.

She said, pointing, "Follow the wall another
twenty yards back. You'll see my tracks. Turn off
and follow them. There's a dry wash where you see
those cottonwoods. You'll be out of sight all the
way. The road dips into the wash farther up, this
side of where you caught up to us last night."

"Hang on," Rhianon said.

The slope down to the wash was easy enough,
but the wash itself was strewn with boulders and
deadfall. It angled off roughly north and east from
the town, the cottonwoods and smaller growth at
its banks making a natural cover. Gunfire still laid
its wicked echoes over the land; it slackened suddenly and then there was another sound that
brought Rhianon's head up.

Wellington said, lifting his voice over the racket,

"Well, that's the door! They'll be riding after us in a few minutes."

"My guess is no," Rhianon answered. "They don't know about the wagon. They'll start searching the buildings. That will take them a good half-hour. After that, they'll start cutting for sign." He turned to Lawney Bevins. "You said something about the horses?"

She nodded. "I was going to untie them and stampede them out of town. Then I knew Colvig and his men would see them and realize you were reckoning to be chased. So I went into Spurlock's and bought a pair of pinking shears."

Rhianon said, baffled, "Pinking shears?"

"Can you imagine," she asked seriously, "a man so greedy that he keeps open for business while all that fuss is going on?"

Rhino Colvig wore the confident glow of a general who knew his troops were placed rightly and that victory was in the grasp of his hand. He had forced Spurlock and the others to ask Wellington and Rhianon to give up the prisoners, this gesture putting the blame upon the other side. Patch and Parsons were placed at the ends of the alley that ran between the buildings and the old mission wall. Nobody could escape that way, and they didn't have any horses anyway, Rhianon's black having been led away. His own horses were on the other side of the Coffin, out of the line of fire. Two men, Ed Peshaur and Con Walsh, were on top of the rock where they could cover the whole area with their fire. Colvig himself made a temporary command post by the Coffin's head where he could signal to both groups.

The townspeople were out of the way, wanting to have nothing to do with this, although doing nothing to prevent it. Most of them had simply bolted their window shutters, barred the doors, and written the day off. Except for Josh Spurlock who, taking a look at Colvig's mended reins, had tried to sell him new ones of latigo leather.

Colvig leaned against the rock, took tobacco and paper from a pocket, and rolled a cigarette. He had just finished twisting the ends when he looked up to see the wagon approaching. It was the Bevins girl, he noted a moment later, and he frowned and stepped out to intercept her. Just like some fluttery female to come blithely riding in and get herself shot in the rump. Still, she wasn't a bad-looking little piece.

He met her where the street veed around the Coffin, saying, "Sorry, miss. We've got a little trouble here."

She pulled at the reins, looking down upon him. "By the sound of all those guns," she said, "that is one of the finest understatements I've ever heard."

Her attitude nettled him. "Look, the best thing you can do is turn around and ride back. You want to get hurt? Those men in the jail are shooting real bullets."

Her eyes turned round. "What men?"

"Wellington, for one. Him and that Rhianon hairpin."

"Hairpin," she said in a musing way. She picked up the reins in both hands. "Well, I've got my shopping to do."

"Now you just stay put!" Colvig growled. "You had to put your meddling foot right in the middle of something yesterday. Don't try to push your luck. Just turn around and drive back."

She gave him a long, thoughtful stare. "That Rhianon is a troublemaker, isn't he? And, Mr. Colvig, you want him and Third Wellington to give up those prisoners, don't you?"

He said irritably, "I've been trying to tell you that." He had raised his voice over the steady rattle of gunfire. It stopped suddenly, and he found himself shouting and feeling pretty silly.

"I can hear you, Mr. Colvig," Lawney Bevins said primly. "I think I can also help you. If I can persuade Rhianon and Wellington to give up their prisoners, will you let them go in peace?"

Instant refusal was on the top of Colvig's tongue. Then the thought came to him: *Why not?* He could only lose five minutes or so, even if it didn't work. And if it did work, it would save a lot of time and perhaps a few explanations to Qualtrough. Either way, it would be proof that he had tried his best to settle this in a peaceable manner.

He gave her what he felt was an ingratiating smile, winced slightly at the pull of the scar Rhianon had put on his cheek, and touched his hatbrim.

"Pull around to the far side of the rock, Miss. I'll get my boys to stop shooting. You can have five minutes."

"Let us all pray for peace," she said demurely, and put the horses into motion, leaving him standing there wondering just how in hell he had got talked into this.

She parked the wagon near Spurlock's, gave the

nervous horses at the tie-rail there a speculative look, and walked back to the Coffin's head.

The firing had ceased. Colvig said, "You've got just five minutes. No more."

She nodded. "They can go in peace if they give up the prisoners?"

"That's gospel," Colvig said, and almost believed it himself.

"All right," she said calmly, and started across the street.

He watched her disappear into the jail's doorway, then lit the forgotten cigarette and waited. He counted, "Mississippi one, Mississippi two, Mississippi three," and on up to sixty. Shortly before finishing this laborious task for the fifth time the jail door opened, and Lawney Bevins came out, walking very slowly.

When she came up to him, he said, "Well?"

She shook her head sadly.

Genuine indignation overtook Colvig. How could anybody refuse the request of so genteel and pretty a girl? Especially when that Rhianon already owed her a favor for yesterday? Him and that turncoat Wellington deserved anything coming to them. It was shameful, them not wanting to do this in a peaceful way. He watched Lawney Bevins walk back to the wagon, restraining a desire to run after her and comfort her.

The way she said that about let's pray for peace, he thought.

He raised his arms to give the signal to resume firing.

Most of the rest of it, to a point involving considerable later embarrassment, went as planned.

He concentrated the fire on the lone front window of the jail, driving Rhianon and Wellington back to where their own lead could do no harm. He then pulled Parsons off the alley entrance and had him drag up a cottonwood log. Then he took Patch off the alley's other end. The three of them took the log, while Peshaur and Walsh threw down a heavier concentration of lead. It took just four tries to ram the door down.

For the next hour or so, life was just one damn thing after another. They searched every building on that side of the Coffin, including the new three-holer back of the Coffin Saloon. He even had Peshaur and Patch comb the brush on the other side of the old wall, ranging as far as two men could possibly get afoot with a couple prisoners. It wasn't until Peshaur belatedly reported the wagon tracks that Colvig got an inkling of what must have happened, even though Walsh said he'd seen the girl ride out of town.

"Get to the horses!" he yelled, and all five reached the tie-rail at the same time. The next few moments were compounded of such horrendous confusion that Colvig immediately blocked the whole thing out, refusing to believe it ever happened.

Walsh was the first man on his horse, vaulting into the saddle without touching the stirrup. Two seconds later he found himself riding the tie-rail, which promptly threw him. That was the only one Colvig clearly saw, for he was hitting his own saddle just as he saw Walsh's incredible acrobatic feat. His own unrehearsed act was less spectacular, but somewhat more educational; for he suddenly and painfully realized that the saddle had somehow turned the tables and forked him, and that his sorrel gelding obviously hadn't been completely cut and besides had a nervous bladder.

Colvig lay there, his wind completely knocked out of him, as stunned mentally as he was physically, listening to the outraged swearing of the rest of the bunch. The sorrel dribbled a few drops on his left boot, then crow-footed aside. Ed Peshaur crawled out of the way of a kicking horse, came to his knees and gave Colvig a stony look. He raised one arm, gave a wearily sardonic salute, and fell flat on his face.

Colvig turned over on his belly and beat on the wet ground with both fists. Before his mind drew a curtain across the rest, he heard Patch say in a wondering tone, "Both ends of this girth look like a saw blade."

They hit the road to the settlement about two miles out of town, Rhianon driving with Lawney Bevins beside him and Wellington stretched across the wagon bed, his shoulders on Pauncefoote's chest and his boots on Johnny Minstrel's belly. Pauncefoote was taking it quietly, but the kid was twisting his body and making muffled sounds through the gag.

Wellington dug a spur into Johnny Minstrel's navel, and said, "I'd take that off, but there's a lady present." He lifted his body, bracing his elbows on Pauncefoote's ribs, "Any signs on our back trail?"

"Not a one," Rhianon answered. He turned to look again at Lawney Bevins. She was sitting as far away from him as she could get, bracing herself with her feet against the dash and one elbow hooked over the back of the seat. Rhianon found himself regarding her with a profound amazement. How, he wondered, could a girl so set against guns and fighting have the nerve to do the things she did? She was intensely female, and more than necessarily proper. Yet twice now she had barged deliberately into dangerous situations and conducted herself with a coolness that would do credit to the whole general staff of the army. Up to now, he hadn't regarded females as much good for anything, except in certain well-defined areas. The areas were beginning to expand.

He looked back at Wellington, saying, "Everything quiet?"

"For the moment," Wellington answered, and grunted as a rear wheel hit a rock. "All we got to worry about now is getting them to the sheriff at Willcox."

X

IT WASN'T UNTIL after dinner that night that Rhianon realized how completely the world had closed in on him. A few days ago, or maybe it was a thousand years, give or take a few, he was planning to lay aside his guns and start trailing horses with his brother and Miles Brandes. Now Johnny was handcuffed to a wagon wheel cursing him, Miles Brandes lay in a dark borderland between life and death, and Rhianon himself had the feeling that if he unbuckled his gunbelt his ass would fall off.

He set his coffee cup down, lit up the cigar proffered by Colonel Bevins, and tilted his head to hear something Third Wellington was saying. He nodded in agreement, not really knowing what Wellington was talking about, and let his gaze sweep the area.

Cooking fires made scattered bright spots in the gray-green dusk, each of them marking high shape of a Conestoga wagon or the blocky form of a tent. A low murmur of talk ran over the land, punctuated by a child's high voice of a dog's staccato bark. At the camp's perimeter a lantern's pale glow moved away like a limping firefly, then made its way back and was lost in the glow of a fire.

Lawney Bevins was scraping dishes and stacking them on the workbench. She was whistling *Oh, Susanna* in a low tone that made it sound like a dirge.

Colonel Bevins looked across the table at Rhianon and shook his head.

"I know what you're thinking. Her mother and I have reminded her of the saying about whistling girls since she was knee-high to a grasshopper."

Third Wellington came heavily to his feet, threw a wary look at Lawney Bevins, and said in a hoarse whisper, "Which way do I go, Colonel?"

Bevins pointed with his ciagar. "That mesquite clump beyond the second fire."

"I'll never make it," Wellington grumbled, and started off.

Watching Wellington stumble uncertainly toward the camp's circumference, Rhianon let smoke trickle slowly into the still air, and said, "And that's another thing to consider."

Bevins raised his head. "Wellington?"

"I made him lose his job. He can't go back to Coffin Rock as long as Colvig and Qualtrough run the town."

"I remember the first words we had together," Bevins said. "You said you hadn't lost anything in Coffin Rock. I'm wondering how you feel about it now."

"My friend, my brother, my conscience," Rhianon said slowly. "Maybe my whole future."

Lawney came over with the coffeepot, silently filled their cups. As she moved away out of hearing, Rhianon's gaze followed her a moment and then came back to Bevins.

"Colonel, I've been wanting to talk to you about this daughter of yours."

"Short notice," Colonel Bevins said dryly. "You've only met her twice."

"Colonel," Rhianon began stiffly, and paused to make a careful choosing of his words. "Colonel, have you ever thought of using hobbles?"

Bevins chuckled through his cigar smoke. "They don't make them that strong." He leaned forward, gesturing with the cigar. "Her great-grandfather led a brigade at Yorktown. Her great-grandmother hiked up her skirts and handled a twelve-pounder at Bunker Hill. Her grandfather was one of the first on the walls of Chapultepec. And her father—well, Sheridan saw fit to brevet me twice." His voice took on a faraway softness. "And her mother died defending her home against Quantrill."

"Then what," Rhianon asked, baffled, "is all this talk about using peaceful means?"

"Maybe she thinks peace is something worth fighting for," Bevins answered. "Man, I know she took chances; and Lord knows I don't condone such carryings on in a woman. But she's of age, and her mind is her own. If I had been here this morning, I would have tried to keep her from following you. All I can say is that I would have tried."

"Hard for me to know what to think," Rhianon said. "It was no business for a woman. And yet Wellington and I would have never come out of the jail alive without her."

Bevins came to his feet. "Meeting tonight. We've

got to decide whether to try to get a supply train through, or give up the whole settlement project."

"All you need," said Rhianon, "are a few women like your daughter."

"There was only one," Bevins said. He moved over to the workbench, kissed Lawney briefly on the cheek, and said, "This may take a few hours. Doc Feathers will be by to take a look at Brandes. Rhianon, what are your plans for those two prisoners?"

"I'll take Pauncefoote to Willcox for trial. The other one—I don't know about the other one."

"Got Luke Dobie guarding them now," Bevins said. "But he'll be wanted at the meeting. I'll find somebody to take his place on the way over."

Lawney said with a surprising vehemence, "Don't you let them talk you out of taking the wagons through."

"I'll do my best," Bevins said, and moved off.

Rhianon ground his cigar out and walked over to where Lawney stood. He picked up a dish towel, met her questioning look, and said, "It's a poor way to show thanks. I just can't think of anything else now I can do for you."

She said, "I gathered you were offended to accept help from a woman."

He squirmed inwardly and avoided her eyes, not knowing what to say.

"Well?" she persisted.

He swiped savagely at a tin cup, his thoughts racing in a confused pattern. He had known this ordeal was coming. It was easy to avoid while Bevins and Wellington were present, but now that he found himself facing her alone he was in a complete state of panic. He got the dish towel caught in the cup handle and fumbled at getting it free, feeling thoroughly uncomfortable, and wishing he could find an easy way out of this.

She was unrelenting. "Does it destroy the image you have of yourself, Mr. Rhianon? The sun god with the shining star on his breast, blinding the world with his presence, walking always alone against the forces of evil, asking and accepting no help?"

He gave the towel an angry yank, freeing it. "You're getting a little rough. I came over to say my thanks. All you had to do was give me a simple welcome."

"I deserved that," she said quietly.

"Friends?" he asked.

"Friends," she answered, and smiled up at him.

Third Wellington returned at that moment, making more noise than necessary. He said, "Think I better have a look at my prisoners. Rhianon, you don't really want that kid brother of yours taken to the county jail, do you?"

Lawney Bevins turned swiftly. "Brother?"

"Oh, hell," Wellington said dismally. "I done it."

"All right," Rhianon said calmly. He brought his steady gaze to Lawney's startled eyes. "That boy Johnny Minstrel is my brother. He's the reason I came to Coffin Rock."

"I see," said Lawney slowly. She looked at him and spoke to him as though Wellington wasn't there. "You didn't want him to go back to Colvig and his bunch of gunmen. I wondered why he was so important to you."

"I know what living by your guns can do to you," Rhianon said.

"Have you talked to him?"

He shook his head. "Not yet. Tomorrow, when he cools down.

Wellington said, "Well, I'll be in the tent," and left.

Lawney turned up the wick of the lantern hanging at the tent fly and came back to Rhianon, very still and very sober. She said quietly, "Dishes still have to be done."

When they were finished, she threw out the dishwater, dried her hands, and took Rhianon's arm.

"Walking is good," she said, and moved him away.

They stayed within the camp perimeter, passing wagon after wagon in silence, the glow from dying fires bringing a warmth to the night's cool darkness.

Lawney said finally, "There is more that you're holding within yourself."

"Yes," he said, and he told her of the child that died that gunsmoke-filled day on the streets of Tombstone.

She listened without interrupting, but her grip on his arm tightened. When he was finished, they walked a while without speaking. They had almost circled the camp; he paused to take tobacco and papers and make a cigarette.

She said then, "Others have forgiven you. Now you must learn to forgive yourself."

He brought the cigarette to his mouth and lit up. The match flame threw hard shadows over his face, making his angular features take on a harsher cast.

He flicked the match out, pinched the end carefully, and ground it under his heel.

"Forgive myself?" he said.

"Yes. I don't mean make excuses—like telling yourself the bullet maybe wasn't yours. Things like that. You must face what happened and take the full blame. Then you must forgive yourself. Don't you see what I mean?"

"Not yet," he said.

"You will," she told him, and took his arm again. "Someday you will."

Doc Feathers was waiting at the wagon for them when they returned, his straw skimmer making him seem strangely out of place among the wagons and tents.

He said in a quietly irritated voice, "Come to see a patient, and everybody's out sashaying around."

Rhianon said, "What do you think?"

"He has a chance to live. Nothing more. Why don't you ask him how he feels?"

Rhianon raised his head quickly, emotion coursing throughout his body. He said in a voice that was like a cry, "Miles is conscious?" and with long strides started toward the rear of the wagon.

"Make it short," Feathers warned, and led Lawney Bevins toward the coffeepot.

A lantern hanging from a wagon bow made a dim light. Rhianon moved farther into the wagon, saying, "Miles? Miles?" in a wondering tone.

Miles Brandes' voice, very small and weak, came from almost underneath him. "Just don't step on me, will you?"

Rhianon knelt, reaching out a hand, feeling he must touch Brandes as well as see him.

"You sound mean as ever."

"Meaner," Brandes said. "Will, I—I don't remember."

"Don't try," Rhianon said. He looked down at Brandes, fighting to keep from betraying his thoughts. Most of Brandes' head was bandaged; one arm was bound in a splint.

"Pauncefoote," Brandes said slowly. "I remember him."

"He'll pay. We've got him cuffed to a wheel."

"Save him for me," Brandes said in a fierce whisper. "Have you seen Johnny yet?"

"I've seen him."

"You don't sound like it did much good."

"Not yet," Rhianon said.

"Just a fool kid," Brandes said. "He'll come around in time." He raised his head from the pillow, this with such evident painful effort that Rhianon drew in a sharp breath.

"I can move something, anyway," Brandes said wryly. "Will, how am I doing?"

"You're in good hands," Rhianon said. "Lie still and let yourself mend."

Brandes' head fell back. "Lots to talk to you about," he murmured.

"Tomorrow," Rhianon said. "Good night, Miles."

Climbing back out of the wagon, Rhianon was more depressed than he had ever been since Brandes was injured. This, too, he thought, was his own fault. Everybody who came close to him seemed to end up hurt in one way or another. He had driven his brother farther and farther along the wrong fork of the trail. Miles lay injured and crippled for life. Third Wellington was out of a job, and with no place to go. And his continued presence here, he knew, could only mean more trouble for Bevins and the other settlers. The obvious thing was to leave as soon as possible. Yet, now that his life had become bound so closely to these others, his leaving would be betrayal.

There was no answer, no way out.

Engrossed so deeply in this somber thought, he entered into the cooking tent's soft sweep of light before he realized where he was. Doc Feathers was already gone, but Lawney Bevins was still there, her eyes laying a sober regard upon him.

She said softly, "You look like a man who has just seen all of the world's darkness."

"Made by my own shadow," he said.

As he turned to look fully at her, hoofbeats made a quickening roll on the dark drum of the night.

XI

Colonel Bevins swung down from the saddle with the definite motion a cavalryman never loses, wrapped the reins around a mesquite branch, and strode into the pool of light. He wore a look of grim exultation; he smote one palm with a gloved fist, keeping this up in a quick rhythm as he approached Lawney and Rhianon.

"We're going to do it," he said.

"When?" Lawney asked.

"Starting at daylight. Three freight wagons, four Conestogas." He turned to Rhianon. "You want to get that man to Willcox, this is your chance. We'll pick up supplies there, then stop at Morse's sawmill on the way back and pick up lumber." He paused, then continued in a thoughtful voice, "If we even make it that far."

Rhianon said, "You've got two-three weeks before the rains."

"Not the rains I'm worried about." Bevins peeled off his gloves, took a cigar from his pocket, and lit up. "We've tried this twice before, and been ambushed both times. A man killed, two wounded badly. Both times after we left Morse's on the way back. Wagons and mules lost, as well as the supplies and lumber. Well, this time we'll take enough men and guns to fight our way back!"

Rhianon said, "Would you recognize any of the bunch?"

"No. They hit us at dusk. Dressed like Indians and yelled like Indians. But they weren't Indians. I've a guess Qualtrough has been rebuilding Coffin Rock with our lumber."

"Better than a guess. You might find a few maverick Apaches ramming about the Chiricahuas, but not enough to raid a wagon train. Curly Bill, Ringo, and that bunch operate strictly in the San Simon. They wouldn't be interested in lumber or flour, anyway. I gather you don't go along the San Simon."

"No," Bevins said. "We head almost due west, cut across the tip of the Pedregosas, up the Tex Canyon trail to Rucker Canyon, and out into Sulphur Springs Valley near the tip of the Swisshelms. Then straight up along the east side of the Squaretops to Willcox."

"Same way back?"

"Except for turning off into West Turkey Creek to pick up the lumber. It's been on the trail from there back to Rucker Canyon that we've been ambushed."

"There's your answer, then," Rhianon said. "Change your route."

Bevins gave him a surprised look. "That would mean the San Simon."

Rhianon nodded. "Right. Follow the east side of the Chiricahuas. They start angling westward about at Galeyville. Then cut through Apache

Pass, head through Dos Cabezas and on to Willcox."

Bevins said dryly, "Kind of like jumping from the frying pan into the fire, isn't it? Qualtrough and Colvig are bad enough—I've no desire to tangle with Curly Bill and his bunch." He drew on his cigar, discovered it had gone out, and fumbled in a pocket for matches. "You outlined the trail going to Willcox. Let's assume we have no trouble. But how about the return trip? We still have to go into Turkey Creek for our lumber. Only way in is from the Sulphur Springs side. And as far as I know, that's the only way out. We'll still have that stretch between Turkey Creek and Rucker to sweat."

Rhianon said quietly, "Getting those supplies and lumber back worth a gamble?"

Bevins gave him a narrow look. "Unless we do, we'll have to give up the whole settlement project. I've talked to the railroad people. I know they'll build through our town—if we give them a town to build through. Otherwise, they'll go through Coffin Rock. And with Qualtrough running things there, we wouldn't be able to ship a peck of anything."

Lawney Bevins, who had been listening quietly in the background, broke in, saying: "I can tell by the look on Mr. Rhianon's face that he's wondering just what we're planning to ship."

Bevins snatched the cigar from his mouth. "Hell, man, I thought you knew!"

"Never thought to ask," Rhianon said in a mildly apologetic tone.

"Fruit," Bevins said. "This can be a great orchard country. Peaches, pears, plums—even citrus fruits." He flung an arm out in a wide-sweeping gesture. "Water lies under this whole San Bernardino valley. Dig almost anywhere and you'll have an artesian well. John Slaughter is already doing it on his ranch. Give us a few years and this will be the orchard of the west."

Lawney said with gentle humor, "That's just the start of the speech, Mr. Rhianon. Later on, he'll get to pomegranates, papayas, and persimmons."

Bevins said imperturbably, "Also cotton. For bed ticking."

"I'll look in on our patient first," Lawney said. She kissed her father's cheek, gave Rhianon a murmured "Good night," and left.

Bevins looked after her a moment, then brought his attention back upon Rhianon. "Let's hear more about this gamble."

Rhianon moved closer to the lantern's yellow pool of light. He hunkered down and picked up a mesquite twig, tracing in the dirt a design that looked something like a scythe. "The Chiricahuas. West Turkey Creek here. Galeyville here. Morse's mill is about at this point." He drew lines across the scythe as he talked. "Going from Tombstone across to Galeyville, you go up West Turkey, skirt along Barfoot Peak, then over Onion Saddle to Galeyville. Worst stretch will be from Morse's to the saddle where Pinery Canyon runs into Onion Creek. But there's a trail, and wagons with enough mules pulling can make it."

Bevins frowned and shook his head. "First objection—disallowing the second for the time. Qualtrough will know we're at Morse's. He can ambush us anywhere between there and Galeyville."

"Uh-uh," Rhianon said. He swept the mesquite twig in a wide circle around the cross he had marked to designate Galeyville. "This is Curly Bill country. Even Qualtrough wouldn't dare stick his nose in there."

"Bringing up the second objection," Bevins said, and gave Rhianon a quizzical look.

Rhianon pushed his hat back and with the mesquite twig began making aimless marks in the dirt. "I came to Tombstone as a deputy sheriff under Johnny Behan. That was just before Curly Bill killed Marshal White. It was an accident. Curly was giving up his gun. White grabbed it and pulled the trigger himself. I was there. The Earps wanted him hung. I testified it was an accident, and Curly Bill was freed."

"I see what you're aiming at," Bevins said.

"Curly and I stayed on opposite sides of the fence. But he said he owed me one favor."

Bevins said doubtfully, "Rhianon, I don't know."

"Chancy," Rhianon admitted. "And it was a long time ago." He flipped the twig away and stood up. "Try it this way. Take your regular route up to Willcox. I'll go along with you and deliver Pauncefoote. The freight wagons will turn off at Turkey Springs and wait at Morse's for us to pick them up on the way back. I'll go straight on to Galeyville from Willcox and talk to Curly Bill. Then I'll cut across to Morse's and let you know. If Bill stands by his word, we can cut across the mountains over to the San Simon. If not, we'll take our chance in the Sulphur Springs."

"That's worth trying," Bevins said instantly. He strode to the bench, picked up his gloves, and slapped them against his leg. He turned then to give Rhianon a look steady and intent. "If this weren't in my camp, it wouldn't be my business. I saw Wellington on the way back from the meeting. I'm wondering what you intend to do about your brother."

"Your right to know," Rhianon said evenly. "I'm like to have him held here until we get back. Right now he won't listen to me. By then, I hope he'll be cooled down enough so he will."

Bevins started to turn to his horse, then paused, and said, "We'll need most of the men with the wagons. I wonder if there will be a try to free him?"

Rhianon considered this question, then shook his head. "You can't take a train over to the Sulphur Springs without everybody in Coffin Rock knowing about it. I'll be with you, and they'll take it for granted we'll have both Pauncefoote and Johnny with us." A sober thought came to him then. "Chances are they'll jump us on the way to Willcox. Colvig won't want to give up easily."

"The possibility has occurred to me," Bevins said.

"And you said nothing," Rhianon said in a wondering way. "Colonel, this can put your future and that of all these other people in jeopardy. I'll have to find some other way to get Pauncefoote to Willcox."

"Nonsense," Bevins said. He strode to his horse, picked up the reins and stepped into the saddle. He reined his horse into the circle of light and gave Rhianon a shrewd look. "You're thinking of bringing Pauncefoote in on your own. That would be a foolish thing."

Rhianon said, his voice holding no conviction, "Perhaps."

Bevins said, "Sleep fast—we'll be up and moving before dawn."

Rhianon watched Bevins break the light's circumference and pass into the darkness, his mood utterly somber. Qualtrough was an unknown factor, but he could not see Colvig passing up the chance to free Pauncefoote. And Johnny Minstrel. Thoughts stampeded through his mind as he blew out the lamp and walked through the night to the tent he shared with Wellington. With luck and planning, the train could avoid attack on the way back. But a successful raid on the train during the passage to Willcox would be just as disastrous as one on the return trip.

He tried to put himself in Colvig and Qualtrough's place, thinking as they would think. Qualtrough was greedy enough to discount attacking an empty train. He would rather wait until it was loaded with supplies and lumber, and then make his move. And it was doubtful that he would care enough about either Pauncefoote or Johnny to make an attempt to rescue them.

Colvig, though, was another matter. He had been beaten and outsmarted. And right now he was probably nursing a rage close to the bursting point from the tongue-lashing Qualtrough had no doubt given him. As soon as he found out a wagon train had started from the settlement, he'd be certain that Pauncefoote and the kid were with it. He would have to ride out without Qualtrough's knowledge, perhaps taking one or two men with him, stalking the train until he saw his chance.

There wouldn't be enough for a full-scale attack on the train—Qualtrough probably picked up extra men from the drifters who hung around the rustler's hangouts in the valley.

Rhianon pushed aside the tent flap, found his soogans in the darkness, and listened incredulously to Wellington's soprano snoring. He started to take off his boots, but his mind was too wound up for sleep. He fumbled for tobacco and papers and stepped outside again.

Lighting up, he wondered how accurate his thinking was. There was a time when he would have never doubted it. He realized now that had been because there had been only himself to consider. Now he found himself involved in the lives of other people. And although this realization came as a shock, he found it not altogether unpleasant. He thought, *Is that what has been missing all these years?* and stared into the darkness, his cigarette forgotten.

He thought then: *I've heard of Qualtrough, but I've never run against him. Suppose I'm wrong about him?* There was the possiblity that Qualtrough would feel he must show his strength to Coffin Rock. Two of his men had been jailed, and the rest of the gang hadn't been able to free them. Once they were in custody in Willcox, there would be no chance to free them. With hard riding, he could round up enough men to attack the train before it reached Willcox.

The thought of Miles Brandes lying broken on the dusty street came strong upon him then. Whatever else happened, Pauncefoote would have to pay. And Colving and the rest of the bunch who laughed as they watched this man being crippled for life. But first, Pauncefoote.

He threw away the unlit cigarette, flicked the hammer thong free of the spur, made a swift adjustment of his gunbelt, and made his way in the night's still blackness towards the wagon where the pirsoners were held.

The wagon loomed up ahead of him, silhouetted against the light of a fire that glowed brightly behind it. Rhianon circled around to the wagon's other side, making no effort to soften his footsteps, and stepped deliberately into the ring of light.

A man's voice said quietly from the farther darkness, "Just lift your arms up and turn around quiet-like, mister."

Rhianon obeyed, saying in a low voice. "You know who I am."

Luke Dobie came into the light, a Winchester held easily. He said in a relaxed voice, "Rhianon," and let the muzzle of the Winchester drop.

Rhianon motioned toward the wagon. "Behaving all right?"

"Bitter, but behaving," Dobie said. "At least good enough so we figured it would be all right to uncuff them from the wheels and let them crawl into the wagon to get some sleep."

"How long until you're relieved?"

"Midnight," Dobie said. He looked up at the slow-turning wheel of the stars. "About another three hours."

"Take a break," Rhianon said. "I'll stand the rest of your guard for you."

Dobie said hesitantly, "Don't know what the colonel will say."

"I'll speak for you," Rhianon said.

"Why, now," Dobie said, "I'm obliged to you. Kind of scary work anyway." He cradled the Winchester and moved off, adding, "Pot of coffee on the fire."

Rhianon waited until his footsteps receded into the night, then started kicking dirt upon the fire. When it was smothered, he drew his gun and stepped to the wagon.

XII

THE WILLCOX-ANIMAS stage raced into Coffin Rock a good two hours late, pulling up briefly at the Lost Coon Hotel to discharge its lone passenger, and immediately continued toward its way station farther up the valley. Pride Qualtrough, all his joints painfully stiff after the twenty-four hour ride, swore meaningly into the cloud of dust, picked up his carpetbag and headed directly for the Lost Coon's bar. The spine-racking ride had already put him into an irritable mood. Before he was half through his first drink he was in a towering rage.

His first thought was to send for Colvig. Then he changed his mind and had a horse brought to the hotel, thinking it just as well that Colvig stay out of town for a while. The hour in the saddle added to the long punishment of the stage did nothing to help his temper; he called Colvig out of the bunkhouse without bothering to dismount and gave him a tongue-lashing that lasted a full quarter of an hour and never slackened in its force.

Rhino Colvig, his face reddened, finally managed to say, "Well, dammit, Pride, you don't know this Rhianon."

"I've never met him face to face," Qualtrough said. "But I know who he is and what he is. You damn fool, why did you have to try to even an old score? Why couldn't you have just kept your mouth shut and let him finish his business and ride out of town?"

"He was up to something," Colvig protested. "That drifter was spying something out for him. Sammy at the stables saw them talking together."

"About what?"

"Sammy couldn't get close enough to hear all of it. But he heard our names mentioned." He lifted both hands in a palms-up gesture. "So I figured we'd teach the drifter a little lesson."

Qualtrough's mouth was a long savage line under his trimmed black moustache. He shifted his weight to the near stirrup and dismounted, throwing the reins to Colvig.

"Do you realize just what the hell you've done? Those town people could put up with a little hurrahing, as long as they saw the money coming in. But slinging lead at the jail is something else. They've already started doing some thinking. That's just one thing. Now Pauncefoote and Minstrel are going to be taken to Willcox and tried. That means they'll be on the stand under oath. Do you think either of those hired guns is going to be loyal enough to keep their mouths shut?"

Colvig said, "Pride, I—"

"Goddam you," Qualtrough cut in viciously. "I've worked a year on this deal. I've spent my whole life waiting for the chance. And now it's close to being ruined because of one stupid gun-happy son-of-a-bitch." Anger mounted in him, pitching his voice to a razor sharpness. He stepped

forward and brought the back of one hand force-
fully against Colvig's cheek.

Colvig staggered back, saying, "Pride, now listen!"

"Shut up," Qualtrough said, and hit him again.

Colvig stood his ground this time, shaking his
head in a dazed way. He realized he was still holding the reins, and dropped them. The horse fiddle-
footed sideways and wandered toward the corrals.

Qualtrough, his eyes narrowly wicked, said,
"You want to try it, Rhino?"

Colvig shook his head. "I'm not that much of a
fool," he said. "Not against you."

"I should kill you," Qualtrough said in a dis-
passionate voice. He let out a long breath. "All
right—no use crying over spilled milk. Time to
mend fences. Rhino, you're fired."

Colvig said, "Pride, I swear—"

"That's how it has to be, my friend. I've got to
apologize to those suckers in town, tell them I
made a mistake in hiring you but you are no longer
in my employ. It's got to be done quick and it's got
to be done good. In the meantime, there's a job for
you."

Colvig said slowly, "I'm getting confused."

"Pauncefoote and Minstrel. I don't want them
to be turned in at Willcox. Rhianon and Wellington will either take them alone, or they'll wait until
a supply train starts. Bevins and his bunch of settlers will have to try another trip before the rains.
Find out what the plans are, and stop them. I don't
care how you do it, but stop them."

Colvig said, "Thought you said I was fired."

"Officially you are. You're not on my regular
payroll anymore. But get Pauncefoote and

Minstrel out of the hands of the law and you'll have five hundred dollars in your pockets."

"I'll need a couple of the boys."

"With what work gets done around here," Qualtrough said, "I won't miss them." His stomach rumbled and he realized he hadn't had a meal since early breakfast. "Who's cooking?"

"Parsons."

"Tell him to get some chow on. Then we'll see what plans we can work out."

Afterwards, their bellies filled, they sat long in the cook shack. Qualtrough was a man who had pulled himself by the bootstraps out of more than one sticky situation. He had no doubt that he could do the same this time. His rage at Colvig had vanished by the time he got his food wolfed down, for he had known Colvig for what he was before he hired him. He listened abstractedly to what Colvig was saying, not really hearing him. Nothing Colvig came up with could ever be any good. But it gave Qualtrough a chance to do some thinking of his own, and after he finished his second cigar he knew what would have to be done.

Colvig said, "Well, what do you think of that idea?" and when Qualtrough didn't answer, he repeated the question.

"Only one way to handle it," Qualtrough said.

"What's that?"

"Kill them." Qualtrough came to his feet, tossed his coffee cup into the pan. "They can't come back here, even if we rescue them. We can't let them shoot off their mouths in front of a jury. So we've got to kill them both."

Colvig said doubtfully, "Going to take a little doing. We don't know nothing except they're being held at the settlement."

"We'll know. I sent Walsh over there to do a little scouting. He ought to be back before midnight."

"Near an hour," Colvig said.

"Get some sleep," said Qualtrough. "You're going to have a busy day." He started for the door and then paused, some vague outside sound holding his attention.

A horse's impatient nicker rose into the night; saddle leather creaked, and bootheels made a muffled thump upon the ground over the hard jingle of spur chains.

Colvig said, "That buckskin of Walsh's. He always—"

"Too soon for Walsh," Qualtrough snapped. He reached the door just as it was thrown back, and had to take a quick step out of the way.

Con Walsh, his oddly wrinkled face red with excitement, burst into the cook shack, coming within an ace of running headlong into Qualtrough.

Qualtrough, grabbing Walsh's arm, said coldly, "What the hell you doing back here?"

"Picked up a passenger," Walsh said, and jerked his head at the door.

Linus Pauncefoote, hatless and looking as though he'd been spending the night fighting wildcats, closed the door behind him and headed straight for the coffeepot. He tipped the lid back and gulped scalding coffee straight from the pot, then swiped a tattered shirtsleeve across his mouth and said, "Who's got tobacco?"

Colvig silently tossed him a sack of Duke's while Con Walsh's curiously high-pitched voice ran on.

"Pride, I was about three-quarters of the way to

the settlement when I saw somebody stagger out of that dry wash near where the old Indian camp was. Didn't know who it was at first, natural like, so I reined my buckskin into a mesquite clump and waited. Then—"

"That crazy buckskin of his nickered, like he always does," Pauncefoote cut in. "Knew who it was right off."

Qualtrough said to Walsh, "Better take care of your horse," and stared after him until the door slammed. He waited for Pauncefoote to get his cigarette built and lit, and presently said: "How did you get away, and where's Minstrel?"

"Didn't, and don't know," Pauncefoote said. He threw a leg over the back of a chair and sat down. "Listen to this, Pride. Listen carefully, because it don't make any sense. They had me and Minstrel handcuffed in a wagon. A guard watching all the time. We were dead asleep when this Rhianon comes to the wagon and pokes us awake with a sixgun. Then he marches us off to a tent, gets the handcuff keys from Wellington, and takes the cuffs off. Not a damn word from him. Wellington took me out of camp, pointed out the North Star, and told me to start walking. I wanted to circle around to the picket line and steal a horse, but he rode herd on me a couple miles or so. Nothing else to do but keep putting one foot in front of the other and hope I was heading the right way. Wasn't long before I run into Walsh."

"How about Minstrel?"

Pauncefoote spread his hands. "Don't know. My guess is Rhianon did the same with him. If he's lucky, he'll be showing up along morning."

"Why?" Qualtrough said softly. "Why?"

"Picked up a few odds and ends," Pauncefoote said. "One thing, Bevins is taking a wagon train up to Willcox. Starting in the morning. I figured they'd be taking me along to turn me over to the county law there. And there must have been something between Minstrel and Rhianon once. That kid hates him more than Rhino ever did."

"Some doubt there," Colvig grunted.

Qualtrough said, frowning, "Rhianon going with the train?"

"Heard one of the guards say so." Pauncefoote ground the finished cigarette under his heel and immediately began shaping another.

"No reason for it," mused Qualtrough. "Wellington could deliver prisoners himself. Why Rhianon?" He shot Pauncefoote a quick look. "That friend of his die?"

"No. Leastwise not yet."

"So he isn't sending a body home." Qualtrough strode to the shack's other side and back again. "Think he let you go for whatever reason, but is taking Minstrel?"

"Be the opposite way, if any," Pauncefoote protested. "I'm the one dragged his friend. The kid didn't do a damn thing but back away from him."

"Didn't think you were in a position to watch," Qualtrough said dryly. "Rhino, what about that?"

"Couldn't understand it," Colvig said. "Ever since the kid's been with us he's been aching to get a gun rep. And he's fast. As fast as Rhianon, maybe faster. When it came to the showdown he just backed against the wall and looked sick. Not yellow—it wasn't that kind of a look. Just like it was something he couldn't make himself do."

Qualtrough shrugged. "Buck fever. All right, the

hell with the kid. If he gets back, fine. If not, he won't be missed much. Rhino, you know what to do. Contact the wild bunch that hang around the Squaretops, and tell them to get ready to play Indian again. Pay the same as before." He turned to Pauncefoote. "How many wagons this time?"

"Heard them mention seven. Three for lumber, rest for supplies."

Qualtrough whistled softly, swung his gaze back to Colvig. "This is their big try. We'll need more men. Better swing into the Dragoons and see if you can pick up a few more guns. If not, you'll still have time to try some of the deadfalls in the alley in Willcox. I'll meet you at the usual place—the hill just northwest of Cottonwood Canyon."

"I'm riding," Colvig said, and left.

Qualtrough watched him go out, feeling some better about the man. This was a field where Colvig could be trusted to handle things right. He couldn't plan far enough ahead to make bacon and beans come off the fire together, and he couldn't be trusted to do most things right unless somebody was standing over him. But he knew every outlaw hangout from the Pecos to the San Pedro, and he could talk men into selling their guns.

Pauncefoote tilted back in his chair and said, "What orders for the rest of us?"

"I'll need Parsons and Vermillion to watch things here. Walsh will keep an eye on the settlement camp, just in case anything turns up. We don't know what's happened to the kid, and we don't know if Wellington is going with the wagon train." Qualtrough shook his head in a puzzled manner. "Just what the hell got into Wellington?"

"Must have been chewing on raw meat," Pauncefoote said. "All of a sudden he started taking that tin star of his sort of serious-like."

"Peshaur," Qualtrough said quickly, and snapped his fingers.

"Or me," Pauncefoote said quickly. "Always thought I'd make a fine figure of a law man."

"No," Qualtrough said. "Not after the whole town saw you dragging that drifter at the end of a rope. I'll see Spurlock and the others in the morning and have them pin the badge on Peshaur."

"Leaves me," Pauncefoote drawled.

"So it does," Qualtrough said, and his voice carried a tone that made Pauncefoote look up sharply. "Too risky to have you staying here now. If that man dies, you'll have a murder charge against you. Which means a deputy sheriff or two poking around. For the looks of things, I'll have to give you your walking papers."

Pauncefoote considered this, not liking it. "I can hole up around Tombstone a spell, Pride."

"Uh-uh," Qualtrough said. "Too close." He moved back to lean against the work counter, resting his weight on one elbow. "Leave me alone, Pauncefoote. I'll think of something."

"Sure," Pauncefoote said, and started for the door.

"Just thought of something," Qualtrough said suddenly.

Pauncefoote, his hand on the door latch, turned. He said, "What?" and then his eyes widened.

The bullet smashed into his mouth.

XIII

COLONEL BEVINS gingerly picked a coal from the dying fire and brought it to his cigar. He tossed it back into the ashes and inhaled deeply, his head tilted back and his whole erect shape very still and very thoughtful.

He said finally, voicing his most sober thoughts, "Rhianon, you've done an injustice to the law. Pauncefoote deserves to be tried. No matter what difficulties we might have gone through."

Third Wellington, hunkered down at the fire's other side, said gloomily, "Had dreams of getting all gussied up and leading Pauncefoote up to the Willcox jail with a rope around his neck. Like a conquering hero. Everybody cheering, and the girls from Patty Cooper's strewing horse-nettle blossoms in my path."

Rhianon, pacing slowly at the outside edge of the fire's fading glow, stopped and said, "Colonel, I realize I was wrong. When we brought Pauncefoote here, he became your responsibility. But suppose I had asked you first. What answer would you have given?"

"No," Bevins instantly said.

"Lot simpler if you'd just filled his belly with lead," Wellington said. "Ah, well—my dream is shot to hell anyway."

Bevins stepped to Rhianon and put a hand on his shoulder. "Will, don't think I don't know how hard that was for you to do. That man crippled your best friend. Maybe killed him. He was in your power, and you let him go to make things easier for a bunch of apple farmers. We're grateful, Will. I'm just wondering whether you might not have laid too much of your thumb on the scale of justice."

Wellington came to his feet, grunting, and yawned hugely. "Since I'm the law hereabouts, I reckon I should be the most offended." He slapped at some insect that buzzed out of the darkness. "Hell, I think I am."

Rhianon said, "Want me to bring him back?"

"Pretty poor specimen," Wellington answered. "We can find bigger game."

Bevins threw a look at the stars. "Three or four hours for sleep. Will, what about that brother of yours?"

"I owe you for a horse, Colonel. Johnny wouldn't say a word to me, wouldn't listen to anything I tried to say. I knew he couldn't show his face in Coffin Rock again and that he'd be too ashamed to go back to the Colvig bunch." Rhianon lifted his shoulders in a hopeless gesture. "I couldn't turn him out afoot."

Wellington said, "You pushed him a mite hard, Will."

"Meant to," Rhianon said. "I knew if I could back him down like that he could never go back to that wild bunch. It seemed like a good idea at the

time. Now I know it was the wrong thing. He hates
my guts more than ever."

Bevins said, "We heard a shot."

"The kid pulled—kind of late. Will just took the
gun away from him and the hammer slipped."

Bevins said, "World seems to close the door on
a man at times. But when one door closes, another
usually opens." He bent his gaze to Wellington.
"Without any prisoners to deliver, there's no need
of your making this trip."

Rhianon threw him an odd look, the realization
of what Wellington was going to say instantly striking him. "I rise to applaud what you're about to
say. But this isn't like forking a bronc again after
being throwed."

"Funny thing," Wellington drawled. "I've sort
of got to like walking on my feet instead of my
knees. I'm still Marshal of Coffin Rock. I'm going
back and do my job."

The wagons pulled out in the first cold gray of
dawn, the Conestogas first with the heavy freight
wagons following. Bevins, with his old army tradi-
tions firmly ingrained, preferred mules to oxen.
That meant that grain had to be carried, thus cutting down the payload on the return trip. But the
mules were faster, and there would be no need for
long stops to graze.

Rhianon rode as swamper on the first wagon,
handling the brake and taking over the jerkline
when Bevins had to check the other wagons.
Neither of them had had more than a couple hours
sleep, rising early to get the train into shape and
make sure each wagon had its tar bucket, wagon

jack, and water keg. The grain was split up among the wagons. Bevins carried extra kingbolts, linchpins, augers, lengths of strap iron and other parts in his lead wagon.

They followed the flat grasslands of the San Bernardino throughout that morning, nooning by the water tank at the foot of Snake Gulch. They turned northwest into the Chiricahuas then, lumbering along the torturous trail that cut across into Rucker and out into the Sulphur Springs valley.

"Fifteen men," Rhianon said to Bevins. "How many men were you hit with?"

"Ten or twelve," Bevins said, and turned briefly to look back at the wagons following. "But we had only three wagons the last two times we tried it. They hit us first time while we were camped for the night. We weren't expecting it, and we lost all three wagons. Next time we were hit on the trail. They cut off the two rear wagons, but we managed to get the lead wagon away." He patted the Winchester that rested aginst the seat. "This time we'll do better."

They hit a long downgrade, and Rhianon laid his weight on the brake. "You said Indians."

"Ever seen an Indian wearing an eyepatch?" Bevins said dryly. "No. These hills are filled with all the riffraff running from the law in Kansas, New Mexico, and Texas. They'll hire their guns for a few dollars."

"And Qualtrough furnishes the dollars," Rhianon said. "Well, we shouldn't have trouble on the way up. And if Curly Bill hasn't changed his mind, we'll make suckers out of Colvig and Qualtrough on the way back."

"Let us hope," Bevins said fervently. "This is our last chance. The rains will cut us off until fall. And by the time we get the wagons loaded we'll have used up every bit of cash and credit to our names."

Bevins fell silent, the trail demanding all his attention. Rhianon, holding the brake steady with one foot, wondered what was happening at the settlement and in Coffin Rock. Doc Feathers had looked in briefly at Miles Brandes, then left with a grim look about his mouth. Third Wellington, after wolfing down a hurried breakfast of pan bread and coffee, had caught up a horse and headed for Coffin Rock.

"First thing I'm going to do," Wellington said, settling heavily into the saddle, "is clean out that center cell. Don't worry none about me—I figure Qualtrough will want to patch things up. He'll lay all the blame onto Rhianon here."

"Who deserves it," Rhianon said soberly.

Lawney Bevins had turned from the cookstove and said, "Ah, more of the world's ills on your shoulders. God soon will have nothing left to do."

Colonel Bevins said quickly, "Lawney!"

"He makes me mad," Lawney said tartly, and began a furious attack upon the dirty dishes.

Remembering that remark, Rhianon spent the hours until the night's camp at the Turkey Creek turnoff in a brooding contemplation of what these last few days had done to him. He could still not forgive himself for all the hurts others had come to through him. He had a vague realization of what Lawney Bevins was driving at: he had played God for so many years in trail towns and mining camps that he had come to feel everything that happened was his personal responsibility. Aside from his one long friendship, he had deliberately cut himself off from other men.

Yet, he stubbornly told himself, the death of that little girl was his doing, even if the bullet might not have been from his gun. As was the crippling of Miles Brandes, and the new troubles brought upon Bevins and the other settlers. Not to mention the hatred borne him by his brother. The weight of these thoughts rested upon him with almost a physical pressure, lowering his shoulders, making his spine ache.

Bevins' voice came to him as though from some other far-off world: "You're leaning a little heavy on that brake, Will." He raised an arm and pointed with the whip handle. "Yonder's Turkey Creek. We'll make the mouth of the canyon just about dark."

This part of Sulphur Springs valley was familiar to Rhianon. The route from Tombstone to Galeyville cut across the valley here. Bill Sander's spread would be two or three miles into the canyon, and just north, on the other side of the creek, was B.F. Smith's place. He had stopped more than once to rest and grain his horse in the shade of the huge black oak by the canyon trail.

He said, "Be too dark to ride into Galeyville tonight. I'll leave the freight wagons at Morse's, then had across the mountains in the morning."

"Luke Dobie knows what lumber we need. I'm hoping he can talk Morse out of it."

Rhianon said, "Hope you don't attach any blame on Dobie about last night. No way he could know what was on my mind."

Bevins said, "Wonder if you knew," and getting no response from Rhianon, gave the trail his attention.

Rhianon that next morning waved good-bye to Bevins and took his place with Luke Dobie on the lead freight wagon. This was a far more exacting form of transportation than the Conestoga. The freighters were larger and heavier, and he knew they would need more mules to make the difficult trip across the mountains to San Simon. At Sander's Spike O, Rhianon let the wagons go ahead, and remained to dicker for mules and a horse. He arranged for the mules to be delivered at the sawmill, then saddled and caught up with the wagons before the canyon bent south to Morse's. Ed Morse listened with some skepticism to the plans to haul the heavily loaded freight wagons across to the San Simon, but agreed there was an outside chance it could be done with enough mules and expert drivers.

"Forget trying to get across to Pinery," Morse said. He spat tobacco juice upon the pine needles and shook his head. "There's a logging trail across to the foot of Chiricahua Peak. Your wagons should be able to make that. Then the best thing to do is head north to Long Park. From there on you've got a fair trail up Turkey Creek to Galeyville. Used to be a horse trail across to Cave Creek and out, but your wagons couldn't make it. And you better wait until morning. I can send a man with you as far as Long Park. There are a couple tricky forks you'll want to know about."

Rhianon agreed, knowing the other wagons

would have a four or five day trip to Willcox and back to Morse's.

"Only thing I'm wondering about," Morse drawled, "is why in hell anybody wants to go to Galeyville."

Galeyville squatted on a flat outthrust of land that jutted between two forks of Turkey Creek, facing the broad sweep of the San Simon. Rhianon came upon it from the south, passing the old stamp mill, and riding slowly down the single street. The buoyant life of this town was a thing of the past now, for the shutting down of the stamp mill a short time past emptied the plank shacks and barracks once filled with miners. Buildings still strung out along one side of the street; but on the other side only Nick Babcock's Saloon and corrals lifted weathered planks against the skyline.

Rhianon made straight for the corrals, ignoring the sharp looks of a couple of men sitting quietly on the veranda that ran the length of the saloon. After taking care of the horse, he walked to the saloon's front and entered. The men he had noticed on the veranda were now at the bar, talking earnestly with Nick Babcock who was leaning over the counter with his back to the door.

One of the men jerked his head, and Babcock turned and said with a distant civility, "What'll you have, stranger?" Then recognition flashed in his eyes; he turned briefly, said, "You damn fools!" in a cutting voice, and moved quickly along the bar to where Rhianon stood.

Rhianon, offering his hand, said, "Long time, Nick."

"So it is," said Babcock. He brought out a bottle

and two glasses. "This one is on me, Will." He waited until Rhianon downed his drink, then said in a lower voice, "No star, I see."

"Left it in Tombstone," Rhianon said. "For good."

"There've been a few tongues wagging," Babcock said. He had lived too long in this country to ask a direct question, but his eyes mirrored a wary curiosity.

"When don't they?" Rhianon said. "Nick, is Galeyville still run the same way?"

"Quieted down some since the stamp mill closed, but our old friends are still around," Babcock said in a casual tone. He gave Rhianon a narrowed look. "How far did you throw that star, Will?"

"Not that far," Rhianon said, smiling. "When's the best time to come in and meet old friends?"

"If you're in a hurry," Babcock answered, "there isn't any best time. If you ain't, try dropping in tomorrow evening."

"Time enough," Rhianon said. "I can take another glass of that, Nick."

Babcock poured, then said softly, "Room here. But watch yourself. Things have changed more than somewhat."

XIV

RHIANON'S next two days were compounded of frustration and impatience. Curly Bill did not show up either that first night or the second; and Rhianon, quietly listening to the run of talk at Babcock's and at Jack Dall's Saloon across the street, began to pick up disturbing information about the leader of the San Simon bunch.

Nick Babcock, pouring a drink that second night, put it flatly, "He's got mean, Will. Not like the old Curly Bill, at all. He may have gulched a few Mexican smugglers and dropped loops on a few cows that wasn't his brand, but Curly was a happy-go-lucky cuss. Sure, he was rough. When he played, he played hard. But lately he's got so he spends most of his time in town sitting under that oak out front with a bottle, just waiting to pick a fight with anybody who walks by."

Rhianon said, "Times change—people change. He's watching the wind sweep the old days away, and he can't stop it."

"Maybe," Babcock grunted. "This was his home, much as he would call any place home. Now it's dying, and all we got is a town full of ghosts.

Maybe Curly is seeing the ghosts."

"All of us have our private demons, Nick."

"Just so." Babcock gave him a shrewd look. "Can't help doing a little wondering, Will."

"No trouble," Rhianon said, and finished his drink. "Just want to ask a small favor of Curly."

"Catch him while he's sober, then," Babcock advised, obviously relieved. "After the first bottle he don't recognize anybody—and he hates strangers."

"Which Galeyville seems to draw a few," Rhianon observed.

"Cheap gunslingers," Babcock snorted. "They hear about Curly and Ringo, and they figure this is the last chance to make a gun rep before the old days die. Burying ground is full of them."

Babcock moved down the bar to serve drinks to a couple of wild-looking prospectors, leaving Rhianon moving his empty glass in aimless pattern over the bar's worn surface. When he came back he said, "Funny the town being so quiet these last days. Usually have a half-dozen or so hard-eyed drifters from the Squaretops looking for a fight or an easy dollar. And the fight usually comes easier than the dollar."

"I've an idea why they're scarce," Rhianon said.

"Hell," said Babcock, "Curly wouldn't hire on any of them itchy-fingered gents. Whatever he does, which is none of my business, he's got his own bunch he can rely on." He gave Rhianon a speculative look and said in a low tone, "Some kind of play out in the Sulphur Springs?"

"Nick," Rhianon said softly, "I can see the wheels turning."

"Gears just don't mesh good anymore," Babcock said. "Well, if Curly rides in tonight, you'll have to be up early to catch him before that first bottle gets emptied. I'll call you soon as I know. One more to sleep good on?"

Rhianon said, smiling, "My company a burr under your saddle, Nick?"

"Not wearing that star anymore makes you fair game. And the name means just as much as it used to. I'm tired of wringing blood out of the sawdust."

"Maybe I'll have that last drink," Rhianon said.

Afterward, stretched out on the hard bed, he listened a while to the small sounds of Galeyville's night, sleep's numbing blanket hovering just out of his reach. A lone rider on a weary horse rode slowly along the street and pulled up in front of the saloon; one of the prospectors guffawed loudly; somebody across at Dall's lurched into the street and smashed a bottle against a tie-rail; Nick Babcock's voice, heavily sarcastic, rumbled up the stair well.

After this last sound, Rhianon heard nothing. He fell into a restless sleep, reliving that day in Tombstone. Then suddenly he seemed to be caught up in a vast swirling whirlpool of gunsmoke that bore him down into its faintly defined vortex. He made a panicky effort to fight his way up and out, and found nothing solid to grasp. A darkly weaving tendril of the smoke ripped the star from his shirt and sent it whirling away into the drifting nothingness, a wilding streaking flash of screaming crimson. He found his gun was in his hand. He tried to shoot his way out, but the gunsmoke folded over him and muffled the roar of the shots.

He awoke sweating, Nick Babcock pounding on

the door and calling, "Will Rhianon! Dammit—
wake up!"

He flung himself from the bed and wrenched
open the door. Babcock was breathing heavily;
blood made a long smear on one sleeve.

Rhianon, the gunsmoke not yet completely
faded from in front of his eyes, said: "Nick . . .?"

"You better come see," Babcock said.

Johnny Minstrel pulled away from the settlement, all his thinking thoroughly confused. These
last two days were ones he would just as soon
forget—and he knew he never would. He was at a
dead loss, somehow feeling himself more a prisoner
now than when he was in that cell or handcuffed to
the wagon. There was no question in his mind
about going back to the hangout; he couldn't ex-
cuse his backing down without telling them who he
really was. And that was something he would never
do.

Just why Will gave him a horse and told him to
light a shuck was something that made no sense at
all. He guessed Will just got tired of butting his
head against a stone wall. He wondered briefly
what happened with Pauncefoote. Maybe Will and
that fat lawman figured it would be easier to gun
him down than take him in to Willcox. Whichever
way, it wouldn't be any loss to anybody.

The important question was what to do from
here on. He had a horse, but no gun. And in this
country a man needed both. He reined up, con-
sidering this, squinted into the darkness to get his
bearings, then spurred off at a sharp angle.

He came upon Coffin Rock some three hours

later, having made a bad guess at the trail and losing an hour or more groping through a blind canyon. A gibbous moon washed Hell's Rim with a pale light; the boulders pasted to the rim's steep face threw long shadows down toward the town.

Johnny Minstrel left the horse in the wash behind the old mission wall and made his way afoot to the jail. In a few minutes he came out again, loaded down with a Winchester, a six-gun and belt, and a pocket stuffed with cartridges. The six-gun was his own; he found it stuffed in the bottom drawer of the splintered desk. He strapped it on, feeling less naked. There was no boot for the Winchester, but it was an old model with a saddle ring and he looped one of the saddle thongs through it.

Feeling more cheerful, he set a course roughly west, not halting until the sharp outline of the Swisshelms loomed before him. Later that day, after a two-hour sleep while the horse grazed, he pushed up the valley and drifted toward the Dragoons. Once, looking back, he thought he saw a wagon train making its slow way along the valley's far side, but the distance was too great to tell for sure. With the bare and uninviting rise of the Pat Hills to his front and a glaring hot sun punishing him, he changed his course and swung toward the Chiricahuas, not long afterward coming upon the Riggs home ranch. Here he talked Billy Riggs into a job, and spent two days grubbing prickly poppies and digging post holes at two dollars a day.

With four silver dollars burning a hole in his jeans, he headed into Bonita Canyon, cut over to

Whitetail, and pulled into Galeyville while the evening was still at its shank. Jack Dall's Saloon seemed to be the livelier; he reined up at that place.

He drank a beer because it was more filling, and then bought another because it was cheaper than the hard-boiled eggs Jack Dall kept on the back bar. There was a desultory poker game going on at one of the tables. He wandered over, ran his remaining three dollars up to twelve. Then, feeling expansive, and thinking ten was a good round figure, he spent two buying drinks for the house. Leaning against the bar, the world at this moment his oyster, he heard a group of riders race along the street and pull to a hard-reined halt. He had an idea they were his kind, and when they didn't come in he wandered across the street to Babcock's.

A couple of men who looked like prospectors came out as he entered. They headed straight for the corrals, not wasting time. Five hard-looking men were bellied up to the bar. Light from the kerosene lamp slanted across them, highlighting the dull set of their features, making the harsh planes of all their faces seem engraved with a pinched and dismal savagery. None of them bothered to look up from their drinks when Johnny Minstrel stepped to the bar's near end.

He wigwagged for a drink. The bartender, whom Johnny guessed was also the owner, came up, his eyes showing no welcome, and said, "Nothing but whisky."

"Drinking beer down there," Johnny observed.

"They've bought it all up, kid. Try the whisky."

"Dammit," Johnny said, "I can see a whole case of it on the floor. What the hell do I have to do to get a beer?"

Five pairs of eyes turned as one to give him an irritable regard. The man closest to him said mildly, "Give him a beer, Nick. One." The other four men dropped their attention from Johnny.

Nick Babcock said, "All right, Curly. One." He brought a thick green bottle.

Johnny Minstrel tilted it and drank deeply, opening his throat and letting the whole contents of the bottle pour down. He thumped the empty bottle upon the bar and said, "Another."

Babcock said in an emotionless voice, "Told you only one."

"Who the hell runs this bar?" Johnny exploded. "You or that Curly hombre?"

The man named Curly flicked him a wintery look, turned to spit into the sawdust. He said as to nobody in particular, "Another snot-nose kid. This whole damn country's going to snot-nose kids."

Anger surged through Johnny Minstrel. He took a step back from the bar, his whole face flushed a deep crimson. He felt he should draw, but there was something about Curly's heatless and winkless eyes that unaccountably kept his hand from his gun.

Curly said in a strangely gentle voice, "Give him another beer, Nick," his eyes never veering from Johnny's stiff shape

Babcock said, "Now, Curly—"

"Just give him the beer," Curly said.

Babcock set another bottle in front of Johnny, then moved quickly away.

Johnny smiled thinly. These jokers weren't so tough, after all. Let them know you don't mind throwing a little lead and they back off.

He gave Curly a glance tough and reckless, said

a sardonic, "Thanks, my friend," and raised the bottle.

The shot shattered the whole upper half of the bottle, sending beer splattering onto Johnny's face and neck, shards of glass ripping across to open a deep cut over his temple. The shock of this held him frozen, still holding the jagged-edged lower half of the bottle in his hand.

The four other men instantly doubled up over the bar, their shoulders shaking with huge laughter. Nick Babcock let out a long breath and picked up a bar rag as though he had seen this many other times.

Curly said through the drifting gunsmoke, "Figured you were so mouthy you'd need a bigger neck on that bottle."

Johnny brought the broken bottle slowly down to the bar. Beer dripped from his eyebrows and chin, and a warmer trickle ran slowly from the cut on his temple. He said, "Put that back in leather and try a bigger target."

Curly said over his shoulder, "Boys, he's inviting us to have some gun practice."

Babcock said, "Boys, for crissake."

One of the men laid a gun on the bar and said, "Nick, you just stay put."

The other three moved around Johnny and shoved him back against the wall. His gun was flipped from the holster and sent skidding into the sawdust. He stood there, whitefaced, Curly's gun muzzle a round eye looking straight at his belly. The three men moved back beside Curly.

Curly said, "First one draws blood buys the drinks." The gun muzzle swerved a fraction to the right, and the roar of the shot seemed to extinguish the flame that briefly bloomed. A dark hole puckered the clapboard an inch away from Johnny Minstrel's right ear.

Curly said, "Cape, your turn."

"Keno," Cape Wilson drawled, and fired.

Johnny gave an involuntary jerk as the bullet slammed into the wood just under his crotch. He saw the man left at the bar pick up his gun, give Babcock a quick look, and move up to join the others. Johnny set his mouth in a grim line, judging the distance to the gun on the floor.

Babcock's hands moved quickly under the bar, coming out with a shotgun.

He said, "Curly, that's enough. That's enough."

All five men threw him a quick look.

Johnny Minstrel made his dive for the gun.

XV

THE DEAD MAN was laid out on the bar. Somebody had pulled off his boots and placed a red poker chip over each eye. Except for the dead man, there was nobody in the saloon until Rhianon and Nick Babcock burst from the stair well and crossed the sawdust. At the impact of their boots on the bar-room floor one of the poker chips slid away, rolled unsteadily along the edge of the bar and then fell to the sawdust with a quiet *thunk*.

Babcock hurriedly snatched a white chip from a table and placed it over the dead man's staring blue eye. He said, "Well, we're late. They likely got him hung by now."

Rhianon said, giving the dead man a quick look, "That isn't Curly. Why bring me into this?"

Babcock, already at the door, said, "That favor you want of Curly pretty important?"

"Yes," Rhianon said.

"Then if it ain't too late already you got to do your asking before he finishes hanging that kid did the killing. Because as soon as it's over, Curly will crawl into a bottle and you won't be able to get anything out of him. Horse at the tie-rail. They'll have taken him down the hill to that big cottonwood by the old smelter."

Rhianon rushed past Babcock, giving him a questioning look.

"Uh-uh," Babcock said. "This sawdust castle is all I got. I'll wish you good luck."

Rhianon took the veranda's width in long strides, ducked under the tie-rail. The horse was a bay gelding but looked vaguely familiar in the false dawn's grayness. An unbooted Winchester swung from a rawhide thong. Rhianon swung up and reined the bay around, his bootheels prodding the horse into a racking trot and then into a long lope.

The town's harsh outlines fading behind him, he crossed a bare space, then followed the road through the tall pines, the land sloping downward here to the south fork of Turkey Creek. In a few minutes he raised the smelter. He remembered that the cottonwood lay a gunshot north of the smelter; once on a trip to Galeyville to serve some papers he had seen a man swinging from one of its limbs. He spurred past the smelter, then cut sharply north. The tip of the cottonwood made a narrow dark triangle thrusting up from the mountain's misty purple. The glow of a swaying lantern made it seem to shift.

He reined the bay to a walk, slowly approaching the circle of light that framed the dark shapes of men and horses at the base of the cottonwood, waiting for the challenge he knew would come.

The shapes took on more definite form now. Rhianon could see one man sitting a horse. He sat oddly stiff and straight in the saddle, his back to Rhianon. Another man stood at the horse's head, one hand evidently grasping the cheek strap. Three more, one of them taller than the others by a full head, made a close grouping at the cottonwood's other side, doing something with a rope. Rhianon's horse stepped upon a piece of deadfall, and at this sharp sound all those men instantly jerked their bodies to an alert tautness.

The warning came in flat tones. "Just keep riding on, stranger. This is kind of a private party."

Rhianon said evenly, "Hello, Curly."

The taller man detached himself from the group and said, "Well, I'll be damned. Come on in and join the fun, Will."

The man on the horse tried to turn in the saddle. The reins made a sharp slap against his face.

Rhianon moved his horse into the light, saying, "What's the occasion, Curly?"

"We were having a little fun in Babcock's. Kid took it serious and gunned one of the boys. Babcock pulled a scattergun and told us not to make any more mess on his clean sawdust. So we brung the kid down here." Curly Bill's voice took on an aggrieved tone. "Country's gone to hell. Man can't even have a little funning no more without somebody losing his temper."

"Hate to see anybody hanged without a legal trial."

Curly Bill threw him a sharply wondering look. "You ain't put a star on again?"

"No. Just remembering you didn't used to hold with this kind of thing."

Curly Bill cuffed his hat back. "That was a time ago. No constable in Galeyville since Thompson left, and that J.P. we had got himself shot. Trial's been had. Cape Wilson might not have been much good, but the kid had no call to kill him. Hell, ask Babcock. He saw it."

"Sure," Rhianon murmured. *No trail,* he thought, *is an easy one. Always a fallen boulder or a washed-out bridge—or a questioning fork that leads to strange answers.* He knew by Curly's restive manner and the uneasy looks of the other men that he was unwelcome here. He felt there was something he should do, but could think of no answer. The hanging might be rough justice and illegal, even for this lawless country. But it was none of his business, now that he no longer wore the star. And to try to stop it would merely more likely result in getting himself killed.

He said, making his voice casual, "Rode in to ask a small favor, Curly."

Curly Bill said, "Damn near anything, Will. Just don't try to talk me out of this."

"Different matter," Rhianon answered. He swung down from the saddle, and for the first time noticed the brand on the horse's hip. He knew then where the horse had come from, and he turned his head slowly to look at the slim figure with his hands tied behind his back.

He now understood the meaning of the small nagging wonder that had been picking at him. The man about to be hanged, except for that one startled movement a while back, had made no effort to see who the new arrival might be. It would be natural for him to look and to make at least a silent appeal for help. This one held himself as though he hoped he wouldn't be recognized, as though after hearing Rhianon's voice he was determined not to ask for help.

Rhianon said, "Wonder if I might know who

your rope meat is," and strode easily toward the prisoner.

He looked up into the defiant eyes of his brother.

And he knew he could do nothing to save him without losing the chance to bring the wagon trail over the mountains safely.

Curly Bill said, "Seen him?"

Rhianon slowly shook his head.

Third Wellington spent his first hour in Coffin Rock rehanging the splintered door of the jail, hauling the desk back to its old place, and trying to restore some semblance of order to the office. He gave a moment's profound thought to the idea of cleaning the accumulation of junk out of the middle cell, then decided he would work on that tomorrow.

Coffin Rock was still asleep by the time Wellington dragged a chair out under the wooden awning and settled himself down for a cigar and some anxious contemplation. One of the guns taken from the two prisoners was missing, but he didn't know if it was Pauncefoote's or Johnny Minstrel's. There was a Winchester gone, too, and he couldn't recollect either he or Rhianon taking it.

By the time he mulled this over through the smoke of his third cigar Coffin Rock was stirring. Old Cato Buffum, who ran the Shoo-Fly, was always the first up. He paused with the key to that place in his hand and squinted a long, unbelieving look at Wellington, then slid the key back into his pocket and jogged awkwardly around the Coffin's head.

"I'll have a delegation by full sunup," Wellington mused. He pulled at his derby, looked to see if the shotgun was still beside his chair, and settled himself for a short wait.

They came over, a group of solemn-faced men, while he was debating whether to spoil his breakfast by having another cigar. He ran his eyes over them, not moving from the chair. Horner, looking grim but expectant. Josh Spurlock, his sideburns seeming more ragged than usual. Buffum, shifting weight from one foot to the other. Adam Hunstedder, very thoughtful.

Cap Horner finally broke the ice, saying, "Hardly thought you'd be back."

"Getting so a man can't rely on nothing," Wellington said cheerfully.

Humstedder said, "This isn't easy for us, Wellington. Some of us feel we've been damned fools. We've had a good look at how Qualtrough plans to run this town. We've likewise had a good look at ourselves. We're wondering what to do."

"You try a new town," Wellington said.

Spurlock threw out his arms. "And lose everything?"

"Josh," Wellington said mildly, "how much actual interest you got in that store?"

Spurlock pawed at his mouth. "Hell, you know how it works. Qualtrough freights in the goods. I get a percentage of everything I sell. I take a little in cash. The rest is on paper. Soon's my interest builds up high enough, the store is all mine."

"Qualtrough sells me my beef," Buffum put in.

"Then listen," said Wellington. "Those settlers out beyond Hell's Rim are going to have a town. They've taken a wagon train up to Willcox. This time they'll bring it back. Don't ask me how I know. But you can take my word for it. And when the town gets built, the railroad will build through it. They're going to need businessmen."

Hunstedder said doubtfully, "How long?"

"About four days. Five, maybe."

Spurlock said, "This Rhianon have something to do with this?"

"Might," Wellington answered him.

Horner said, "Easy for me to move. I can even get my building knocked down in that time and move my business, lock, stock, and barrel."

"Different here," Hunstedder said. "Josh and I have stock to move. I figure my share of it comes to about a third by now. Hate to move it with the rains coming."

"Lots of canvas around," Wellington said. "Well, you boys go talk it over. But keep it among yourselves."

Horner said, "Hold it a minute—this is going a mite fast for me. Wellington, you know for sure they'll get a wagon train through?"

"For sure," Wellington said.

"If they get one through, they'll get a dozen," Horner mused. "A new town out from under this damn rim and Coffin Rock will be left high and dry. Worth augering over."

"Among yourselves," Wellington warned again. He fixed his gaze on Spurlock.

"Don't worry about me," Spurlock said hurriedly, and shifted his glance.

Wellington said to Buffum, "Steak and eggs and potatoes ready in about half an hour?"

"No potatoes," said Buffum. "We got hominy."

"What's the use," Wellington said glumly, "of standing on your feet when you have to eat like a hog anyway?"

Wellington spent most of the rest of that day talking to other men in Coffin Rock. Hugh Roybal at the butcher shop and Frank Stein of the Acme Assay Company listened soberly and agreed. Beaver Jones, who ran the Coffin Saloon, had a wife and two children and said he would wait until he knew the wagon train had come through. Price McLean at the Lost Coon Hotel merely threw up his hands, although he said he could see the point in Wellington's argument that there wouldn't be any business in Coffin Rock anyway after the settlers built their new town. The freight company and the Bulldog Saloon were owned solely by Qualtrough; Wellington didn't bother to stop at either one of those places.

All in all, Wellington cheerfully thought, it had been a good day's work.

Pride Qualtrough waited two days before riding into Coffin Rock, allowing this amount of time for its citizens to simmer down a little. He decided to openly admit the killing of Linus Pauncefoote. The story he would tell would even help boost his reputation as a peace-loving man. He rehearsed it in the saddle. Pauncefoote escaped and made his way back to the ranch. Qualtrough was so shocked by the man's horrifying deed that he could not restrain his anger, and told Pauncefoote that he would turn him back over to the law. Pauncefoote then drew a gun, and Qualtrough was forced to kill the man.

After that story, plus a statement that he had fired Colvig, he was sure that Coffin Rock would get over its jitters and forget to question. This last was something that Qualtrough knew could kick the lid off. As long as those people could think of nothing but the profits they were making and would make when the railroad came through, they wouldn't think about other things. Let them start to ask themselves questions and they might come up with the wrong answers.

Colvig's play had been foolish, but there was no use crying over spilled milk. He would make the best of it, and a good con man should be able to make the suckers like it. After all, they should be grateful to him. Coffin Rock had been nothing but a cluster of shacks and a few half-starving people. In a year, he had changed that. And if any of them suspected they were making their profit from stolen supplies, they were smart enough to ignore it. What they didn't know wouldn't hurt them. Anyway, not until later, when they would discover they were no longer partners.

In another couple of days he should have word that Colvig had taken the wagon train. That would put an end to Bevins and his settlement for good. With them out of the way, there would be no question about the railroad coming through Coffin Rock. As soon as that knowledge was final, he would take over all the business enterprises in Coffin Rock. And maybe find a more reliable man to wear the law badge.

Wellington, he mused, had surprised him. But that was because of the meddling by Rhianon. Well, no use worrying about Rhianon again. He wouldn't be back.

He swung the horse around the Coffin's head, then pulled up suddenly, his gaze fixed unbelievably downstreet.

XVI

THE TONE OF the conference at Morse's mill that evening was grim and somber. Colonel Bevins had pulled in with the four Conestogas loaded with flour, salt, hardware and other staple goods, picking up the extra mules on the way up the canyon. His greeting to Rhianon was cheerful, but now his face was set in a thoroughly sober cast. He listened quietly to Rhianon's low-toned talk, looking up occasionally and stroking his moustache.

"So," Rhianon concluded, "Curly Bill owed me one favor. I had to make a choice. And I regret I must say the choice wasn't even hard to make."

"Hard thing to let a man's own brother be hanged," Bevins said. He gripped a wagon wheel spoke and pulled himself to his feet. "Well—what now, Will?"

"We've been working on a plan. I'll let him tell you about it." He turned his head and called, "Johnny!"

Johnny Minstrel dropped the latigo strap he had been mending and came up. His steps were uncertain; his eyes were unsure.

He stopped beside Rhianon and said in a halting

voice, "Colonel Bevins, I don't know how to apologize."

"Don't try," Bevins said instantly. "You're a lucky young man, Johnny Minstrel."

"Rhianon," Johnny said firmly. "It took the feel of a rope around my neck to make me know my name is Rhianon." He gave Rhianon a quick look. "Although when Curly asked if you knew me and you shook your head I figured I'd be hanged as Johnny Minstrel."

"I didn't know you then," Rhianon said gently. "I hadn't known you for over ten years. But now I'm glad I've got my kid brother back with me."

Bevins said, "Will says you've worked out a plan."

Johnny nodded. "I joined the gang too late to be in on the last raids. But I know how they work. Will's original plan was to take them across the mountains, and get Curly Bill to spread the word to all the San Simon bunch to leave them alone. Well—" He hesitated and threw Bevins an apologetic glance. "Anyway, you can't do that now. You got to take the same trail back you always have."

"All right," Bevins said patiently. "What do we do with the wagons?"

"You let them be captured," Johnny blurted.

Bevins raised a shaggy eyebrow. "You mean let them have empty wagons, and leave the supplies and lumber here to pick up later? It's no good."

"Not what he means," Rhianon broke in. "Go ahead, Johnny."

"Thing is," Johnny said, "you're going to lose the wagons anyway. I've heard Colvig say he can pick up twenty-five or thirty men from around the

Squaretops. You can give them a fight, but you'll eventually lose the wagons and probably a few men besides. All right, let Qualtrough freight the stuff in for you. Then take it back from him later on when you've got only four or five men to fight."

Rhianon said, "This makes sense, Colonel. These gunslingers Colvig hires take their pay and head for Tombstone or Willcox to spend it. Johnny knows where Qualtrough hides the wagons and supplies until he thinks it's safe to bring them in."

"There's a park up by the head of Horseshoe Canyon," said Johnny. "Qualtrough waits a month or so, and then sends his own freight wagons up to Willcox. Only he never goes to Willcox. All he does is transfer the stolen supplies to his own wagons, wait around a while, then haul it back into Coffin Rock. You've been buying your own goods from Spurlock and Hunstedder ever since you settled."

Bevins slowly stroked his moustache. "Spurlock and Hunstedder know that?"

"Pretty sure they don't. Unlikely either one would knowingly handle stolen goods. Hunstedder is too honest, and Spurlock too scared."

Bevins turned to Rhianon. "How do you propose to work this out?"

"Like this," Rhianon said promptly. "First, we tandem the wagons. That means we'll only need four drivers. Rest of the men will take the extra mules and head straight back for the settlement. They'll have to cut across the mountains, but on muleback and without any wagons that will be easy. Now, you've always been hit at the same place and during night camp—is that right?"

"Right," Bevins said.

"Chances are then that they'll do it the same way this time. We make night camp at Whitewater Draw. Soon as it gets dark we saddle four mules and have them ready. When they hit us, we'll do enough shooting to keep them from wondering. Then we mount the mules and get out of there. Colvig will have the whole bunch ride with him to the hideout at Horseshoe Canyon, to prevent a counterattack. Then they'll be paid off and leave. One of us can scout the hideout. As soon as we know the bunch has left, we'll take the wagons back."

"That could work," Bevins admitted. "Now, who's going to do the driving?"

"Kind of like to be included," Johnny said quickly.

Rhianon shook his head. "Can't risk it, kid. If you're recognized even Colvig might figure we're running a sandy. The colonel will have to be one. They'd think it odd if he wasn't along. I'll take one wagon, and the colonel can pick a couple more good men."

"Luke Dobie and Ben Wagmen," Bevis said. "Both good drivers, and steady enough not to panic. And, Will, I've got some questions about you driving a wagon. For one thing, none of the rest of us know the Chiricahuas. The bunch going back on mules will need somebody to guide them. The other thing is"—and here Bevis paused briefly—"that if Colvig knows you're with the wagons he won't be satisfied with just capturing them."

"Point there," Rhianon agreed. "All right, I'll take the mules down. We'll head straight down the south fork of Morse Canyon past Buckskin Saddle, then across to Bear Canyon and follow the ridge until we come out north of the Pedregosas. We should get to the settlement a day ahead of you. Better tell your men to keep this under their hats."

"We'll start at daybreak," Bevins agreed. "Wish we could have arranged for some law to come back with us. Deputy at Willcox said our trains haven't been the only ones hit, but there just aren't enough deputies to go around. Meant to mention also that I got a chance to talk to some of the railroad people. No promises, except that they'd come down and take a look before making a decision."

Rhianon said, "Work to do if we're going to get started early. Sooner we get this over and get back to the settlement the better."

* * *

Two days later Rhianon and Johnny with the other nine men jogged their tired mules into the settlement camp. The journey along the spine of the Chiricahuas had been uneventful, but both men and mules were ready for a decent meal and a few hours rest.

Rhianon went directly to the Bevins' wagon, finding Lawney Bevins and Third Wellington waiting for him.

He said, "You don't have to say it. I can tell just by looking at you. When did it happen?"

"The day after you left," Lawney answered. "He went into a coma again. I ran to get Doc Feathers, but it was already too late. I'm sorry, Will. I'm so very sorry."

"Better that way," Rhianon said huskily. "I don't think Miles could have stood riding a wheel-chair the rest of his life."

Wellington said, "He's up on that little rise yonder, Will."

"Thanks," Rhianon murmured, and turned away.

He spent a lonely and defeated quarter of an hour beside the grave of Miles Brandes, thoughts crowding his mind and making him feel very humble and very unsure. He said finally, "So long, Miles," and walked slowly back to the camp.

Lawney Bevins had steak, potatoes, and dried apple pie ready for him. He ate with an appetite that made him feel a little ashamed, listening to Wellington's talk.

"Qualtrough was a mite surprised. But by that time Horner and Hunstedder and some of the others was gathered around, so he took it like a little soldier. Allowed as how he had fired Colvig, then had to kill Pauncefoote. All honey and molasses. Congratulated me on my fine stand for law and order, and told the citizens that you outlanders who'd been trying to drive them from their God-given home and hearth were on your last legs and would be leaving the country. Then he said he had a freight shipment to see about, and he hasn't been back into Coffin Rock since. I'm still some unclear about what's going on."

"This is the way we figured it," said Rhianon, and he told them of the plans made to get the wagons through safely.

When he finished, Wellington said, "Sounds logical, provided Qualtrough gets rid of them twenty or so gunslingers. But suppose he keeps them on?" He waited until Lawney Bevins moved away with the coffeepot, and lowered his voice. "Or suppose Qualtrough figured there must be a skunk in the woodpile and has other plans up his sleeve? The colonel and the others haven't got here yet. Sort of set me to wondering. And I've a hunch Qualtrough rode out to take a personal hand with the wagon train. Otherwise he wouldn't have left two days ago. If Bevins doesn't show up—''

Wellington broke off as Johnny spurred a horse around the wagon and reined up. He said quickly, "Rode north a piece to take a look-see. Spotted three riders on mules. They was leading another mule."

Rhianon said, frowning, "Should have been four riders."

"Only three," Johnny said. "Rode back here soon as I spotted them, so didn't get too close a look. But I'm plumb sure there were only three."

Rhianon came to his feet. "Let's ride out," he said, and headed for the rope corral.

He and Johnny spotted the riders before they were ten minutes out of camp. Johnny was right. There were only three men on muleback. They were strung out single file, the last man leading a riderless mule. The distance was too great to determine who the men were, and a westward-sliding sun made the land waver and play strange tricks upon a man's eyesight.

"Come on," Rhianon said grimly, and put spurs to his horse.

Three riders—and one empty saddle. Rhianon felt icy fingers crawl along his spine.

Johnny, spurring ahead of him, called back, "Last mule is dragging a travois!"

Rhianon narrowed his eyes against the sun. Sure enough, the last mule in line had tree limbs lashed to each side of its saddle, their ends dragging the ground several feet behind. This was an arrangement long in use by the Plains Indians for hauling.

Laced together with rawhide or canvas, the travois made a springy platform. On this one, Rhianon was sure, a wounded man was being carried.

As he wondered which man this might be, the lead rider of the small caravan raised an arm. Rhianon raced past Johnny, and in a moment was shaking Colonel Bevins' hand.

"Wait until I get a square meal and a gallon of coffee," Bevins said, "and I'll tell you about it. Man on the travois is Luke Dobie. Got some lead in his leg, but other than keeping him from forking a saddle, he'll be all right."

They left Luke Dobie off at his wagon, Johnny riding over to the other side of the camp to fetch Doc Feathers. Bevins dismounted with a sigh, stretched, received his kiss from Lawney, and wolfed down his food while Rhianon filled him in on the events of the past few days. Third Wellington added his own comments, then saddled up to head back for Coffin Rock.

Bevins said, refilling his coffee cup, "No way of telling if they suspected anything or not. We made it easy for them, but not too easy. They hit us like we expected, at night, and we triggered off a few shots before mounting the mules and riding off. Luke caught a stray shot, but otherwise nobody hurt. Too dark to recognize anybody, but they were all half naked and yelling like Indians. We were parked where they could only hit us from two sides, and they were still shooting while we were halfway up the side of the mountain. We'd made several cooking fires, dirtied up a dozen tin cups and plates, and tried to make it look like we had a full crew."

Rhianon said, "Any idea how many in the raiding bunch?"

"Spotted them in the morning. Must have been twenty-five or thirty. They weren't taking any chances this time! Paralleled their trail all that next day until we cut across the mountains. Saw a rider come up to meet them near the end of that day."

Rhianon said, "That would be Qualtrough. Wellington said he rode out a couple of days ago."

Bevins shook his head. "Didn't come in from that direction. Don't know the country west of here too well, but I'd guess this rider was heading from Bisbee."

"Doesn't make sense," Rhianon said. "Qualtrough could make it to Bisbee and back to meet the wagon train in that time. But why? Railroad people there?"

"Their offices are in Willcox," Bevins answered.

"Bisbee," Rhianon mused. "Nothing there but miners and the vultures who bunch around to take their pay from them."

"It gives pause for thought," Bevins said.

"Possible." Rhianon looked past Bevins to see a horseman quarter towards them, a bulky shape who bounced in the saddle. It was Third Wellington; he pulled up to a shaky halt, his derby jammed down upon his ears.

"This," he said dourly, "is something you won't believe!"

XVII

PRIDE QUALTROUGH waited impatiently, but growing more and more confident as the long minutes slid by. Running into Third Wellington was pure luck, for this meant he would have to be at a disadvantage by talking to Bevins in the settlement. It was always easier to play a sucker when there weren't a lot of other people around.

The ride in from Bisbee had been long. All his muscles ached, and he wanted desperately to climb down from the saddle and stretch his legs; but he felt it would be better to meet Bevins on horseback. It was always harder to break down a man's stubbornness when you had to look up at him. He moved his gunbelt around, placing the holster at his left side where it wouldn't look so conspicuous. The gun would still be placed nicely for a cross-draw, just in case its use became necessary.

Sheet lightning flashed over the Pedregosas, and a low rumble of thunder rolled over the land. A grimly dark bank of clouds crept steadily over that rugged horizon, like some old god of the range slowly pulling up his blanket. The sun was a dull ball of orange balanced unsurely on the tip of Sunset Peak.

The rains, Qualtrough reflected, should hit within a day or two. That meant that the settlers would have no other chance to get supplies for another month or six weeks. If they had any sense at all, they would agree to his proposition. He had to admit that their plan to get the wagon train through was cleverly worked out. They just hadn't considered that he would ride out to meet it, relying on the fact that Colvig wasn't any too bright. Too bad he couldn't convince all those hired gunslingers to stay with the wagons after they brought them in to the hideout in Horseshoe Canyon. It meant this long ride to Bisbee and back, but taking the wagon train legally made things even better. He wished he had found time to stop in Coffin Rock before riding out to the settlement. He had no worries about his hold over the people there; but after this last fiasco of Colvig's it might be a good idea to smear a little extra salve on their wounds.

Thus thinking, he turned his attention again to the road and frowned when he saw three riders approaching from the settlement. Wellington and Bevins would certainly be two of them. It was his guess the other would be Rhianon.

* * *

Pride Qualtrough didn't at all look as Rhianon always imagined him. It was hard to judge his height in the saddle, but Rhianon guessed him to be under six foot. He was squarely built, with powerful shoulders and long arms; a long drooping moustache tinged with gray gave him an expression more mournful than deadly. He sat his horse with a certain amount of dignity; and Rhianon remembered the man had once been a Justice of the Peace in Las Vegas when that town was ruled by the old Hoodoo Bunch.

Wellington, riding at Rhianon's stirrup, muttered, "That sanctimonious expression could almost make a man believe he's honest."

Colonel Bevins jogged past them and pulled up, waiting for Qualtrough to move forward to meet him.

Qualtrough said mildly, "Asked you to come alone, Colonel."

Wellington drawled, "I was going on back to town, anyway. See you tomorrow." And he spurred on ahead at a racking trot, holding his derby with one hand.

"Anything you can say to me can be heard by Rhianon," Bevins flatly said.

"Makes no difference," Qualtrough said, and shrugged his shoulders. "I'll put it to you bluntly, Colonel. You've lost a wagon train. It was attacked and captured by Indians."

"Some of whom," Bevins said, "had blue eyes and chewed tobacco."

"Luckily," Qualtrough continued blandly, "some of my men happened along later and rescued the wagons. It wasn't their business, of course—but they felt it was the least they could do for a neighbor."

"Just turn the wagons and goods over to us," Bevins said evenly, "and I'll see your men are rewarded for their generous act."

Qualtrough tugged at his moustache and sadly shook his head. "Problem is, Colonel, we're faced with a legal situation. You see, there's a salvage law on the prairie just as there is at sea. Since my men rescued the wagons, they and their contents are legally mine. To make sure no problem can come up later on and that there will be no misunderstanding, the wagons and contents should be impounded and then released through the courts."

Rhianon said, "Or else settle it out of court?"

"That's possible, of course," Qualtrough said gravely. "Now we all know the situation, so there is no point in beating around the bush. I'm hoping the railroad will come through Coffin Rock. You are hoping it will pass through your community. But you will need the supplies and lumber on those wagons before you can build your town. Colonel, I deeply sympathize with you, but I am afraid you are fighting a losing battle."

Bevins said levelly, "What do you suggest?"

Qualtrough spread his arms in a wide gesture. "A simple solution, Colonel. You're beaten, no matter how you play it. But I am not entirely without heart. You haven't time to get another wagon through before the rains. And I imagine you are getting down to the last of your funds. I'll buy the supplies and lumber from you, let you have the wagons and mules back, and offer any of you who desire the opportunity of settling in the growing community of Coffin Rock."

The shoulders of Colonel Bevins visibly sagged. He turned to Rhianon, the question strong in his eyes.

Rhianon, giving Qualtrough a fully penetrating look, said, "I've heard of these salvage cases before. They haven't always been upheld."

"True," said Qualtrough. "But the time involved, the law fees. . . ." He lifted and dropped his shoulders. "Isn't it better to get it settled now?"

"We'll let you know tomorrow," Rhianon said bluntly.

Qualtrough said to Bevins, "Colonel, who's running your settlement? You, or this drifting gunslinger?"

"I'll have to talk to the other settlers," Bevins said firmly. "I'll meet you in Coffin Rock tomorrow afternoon."

"Time enough," Qualtrough agreed. He reined his horse around, then turned in the saddle to thrust home a pointed warning. "Don't let yourself be talked into anything foolish, Colonel."

Watching Qualtrough's shape grow small in the distance, Bevins said presently, "Will, you've got an idea."

"I'm working on one," Rhianon agreed. "Colonel, this salvage angle may or may not hold up. Whether it does or not, you can't afford the time lost in fighting it. But we have an arrow or two in our bow that Qualtrough doesn't know about."

Bevins reined his horse around, heading back toward the settlement. "You'll have to make it plainer than that, Will."

"We've got Johnny," Rhianon said. "And Johnny knows where Qualtrough parks the stolen wagons. And we've got the people from Coffin Rock. You haven't had a chance to go over to the town site; but Horner has already set up shop, and Hunstedder has moved most of his stock out of Coffin Rock. Wellington says they'll all be out of Coffin Rock by tomorrow afternoon. That means that all Qualtrough has now is an empty town. And

I've an idea he won't even have that very long."

Bevins threw him a curious look. "What are you figuring to do, Will?"

"Fight fire with fire," Rhianon said. "We'll hash it over with the rest of your settlers tonight."

The talk that night was long and sober, each man listening intently and adding his own thoughts to the discussion. There were some for recapturing the wagon train at once; but Colonel Bevins pointed out that the train wouldn't arrive at the hideout until tomorrow, and the hired bunch of gunslingers wouldn't leave until then. At Rhianon's suggestion, Johnny and two other men saddled up and rode toward Horseshoe Canyon.

Wagons from Coffin Rock rumbled in throughout the night, Bevins giving each a warm welcome. Even Josh Spurlock eventually arrived with a load of hardware, Third Wellington riding beside him; and Beaver Jones set up a tent saloon just outside the camp. Price McLean of the Lost Coon had already made two trips, bringing what furniture and fixtures he could remove from the hotel. Wellington listened somberly to Rhianon's orders, then immediately rode back to Coffin Rock.

Men left in small groups of twos and threes, each group with a particular job to do, until only six were left besides Rhianon and Bevins.

Bevins came to his feet, saying in a puzzled tone, "Will, we're ready to go along with any plan you make. But what I can't understand is why we just don't go ahead and take those wagons back."

"We'll get the wagons back," Rhianon said.

"But if my way works, we can do it without anybody being shot." He moved closer to the fire, his features seeming to become more square and angular in this light. He waited until the thunder that followed a jagged streak of lightning subsided, then continued. "We'll need five or six wagon jacks. Do you have that many?"

"Should be three, anyway," Luke Dobie answered from the farther shadows. "Rest were with the wagon train."

"Check with Spurlock and Hunstedder, then. You'll need picks and shovels, too."

Bevins said quietly, "Just what are you going to do, Will?"

"We're going to get those wagons back," Rhianon said. "And we're going to end Qualtrough's hold on Coffin Rock forever. As soon as you get those wagon jacks and tools, stop back here at the wagon. Then we'll all get some rest. We'll have aching muscles tomorrow night."

Rhianon and Bevins rode down from the Rim that next day with a pale green-gold ghost of a sun almost directly overhead. Clouds were rolling up, moving swiftly up the valley, and a gusty wind whipped dust into small whirlwinds that ran their own devious courses. They kept to the Rim's east side, out of sight from anybody looking from Coffin Rock, letting the horses have their heads along the long slope that eventually leveled off into the valley.

Here they halted at a small *cienega,* splashed water on their faces and let the horses drink.

Rhianon, after a short wait, mounted up again and rode a way back up the rise. When he returned he had anxious furrows between his eyes and his mouth was set in a grimly straight line.

Bevins said, "Lose something?"

"Johnny was supposed to meet us here and let us know what the situation is with the wagons. He isn't in sight."

"Didn't know about that," Bevins said. "How long can we wait?"

"We can't. Sun's at about its high now, and Qualtrough will be coming in. I'd like to get to Coffin Rock before he does."

Bevins led his horse away from the spring, grunted, "Ho, boy!" and swung into the saddle. "How much difference will this make?"

"I'm not sure," Rhianon said honestly. "It may make all the difference in the world. We'll know in about half an hour, Colonel."

XVIII

THEY RAISED Coffin Rock after a twenty-minute ride, not reining their horses in to a walk until they reached the town's edge. At the Coffin's head they bore right, slowly passing the assay office, butcher shop, Spurlock's, and the other buildings on that side of the big rock. All of these places had their doors closed and windows shuttered. Even the Bulldog Saloon looked deserted.

Circling the Coffin's other end, they arrived at the jail, finding Third Wellington waiting for them.

"What I've always wanted," Wellington said cheerfully. "A quiet and peaceful town."

"Everybody out?" Robinson asked quietly.

Wellington nodded. A drop of rain splashed upon the crown of his derby. He shifted his shotgun to the other arm, lifted his derby off and gave it a shake, then replaced it. "Even the bartender at the Bulldog. Took a little persuading, but I convinced him his best interests lay elsewhere. The freight office was just a front, anyway. Qualtrough never kept anybody there. Human nature is funny. Like cattle on a bed ground. All it takes is for one old steer to get up off his knees, and the rest follow."

Rhianon threw a look up at the Rim, straining his head back until his neck muscles ached. The boulders that were balanced on its top and hung so precariously to its steep side seemed larger than he remembered.

Bevins said quickly, "Riders coming in," and swung down from his horse.

"Leave the horses here," Rhianon said, dismounting. "We'll meet them on the other side of the rock. I want Qualtrough to get the full force of this. And I want to make sure the men on the Rim can see my signal. You have that paper, Colonel?"

"In my pocket," Bevins said, and followed Rhianon and Wellington around the Coffin's head.

They were in front of the assay office when Qualtrough, followed by Walsh and Parsons, loped up and halted facing them.

Qualtrough said with a bland arrogance, "Made your mind up, Colonel?"

Bevins took a folded paper from an inside pocket and handed it to him. "Here's the release," he said, and stepped back.

Qualtrough insolently hooked a leg around his saddle-horn and flicked the paper open. He scanned the paper briefly; then his whole countenance darkened and he threw both Rhianon and Bevins a scowling look that reflected the utter savagery of his thoughts.

"What the hell is this? Goddammit, you said it was a release!"

"It is," Rhianon said evenly. "All you have to do is sign it and turn the wagons over to us."

Qualtrough made a short jerking movement of

his head. Walsh and Parsons moved away a few paces, their eyes never shifting from Bevins and Rhianon. Third Wellington, not missing this furtive movement, walked casually to the street's other side and leaned his bulk against the rock.

"Point is," Rhianon continued in the same even voice, "we're offering you an even deal. You can have your town back in exchange for our wagon train."

Qualtrough gave him a narrow-lidded look. "You're going to have to cut the deck a little deeper, friend."

"I can make it plain," Rhianon said. He moved slowly to the street's middle, took his hat and waved it over his head in a slow arc.

He pointed them to the top of Hell's Rim at a point north of the town.

There was a wait that seemed interminable to him, the seconds crawling by at a frustrating rate. Then the boulder at that place where he pointed moved slightly as though freeing itself from the shackles of ages. There was this slight movement, then nothing more; and Rhianon had his moment of sinking doubt.

The boulder moved outward again, held itself in a gravity-defying position a second, then seemed to tear itself loose from the Rim. Distance seemed to make it move slowly. It staggered down the steep slope in a drunken path, then picked up speed and thundered down, bringing with it a small avalanche of lesser boulders, and was soon lost in a huge cloud of dust. They could hear it strike the valley's bottom a quarter of a mile from the town's outskirts.

Rhianon waited until the heavily reverberating echoes died away, then said to Qualtrough, "This is what we mean. Give us the wagons, and you can keep your town."

Qualtrough reined in his nervous horse and said, "How far do you think the townspeople will let you get with this?"

Wellington's voice soared across the street. "You've lost yourself a town, Qualtrough. You were so tied up with your greed you didn't notice how quiet Coffin Rock is. How many people do you see on the street?"

Qualtrough turned briefly, giving Wellington an utterly wicked look. He spurred his horse to the plank walk, cupped his hands to his mouth, and called out in a voice tense with panic.

"Spurlock! Horner! Buffum!"

"Rest your voice," Rhianon said. "They can't answer."

"A goddam trick," Qualtrough rapped, and flung himself from his horse. He threw open Spurlock's door, cast an incredulous look inside, then walked with quick steps to the assay office. He kicked the door of the place in, growled, "Stein, dammit, stop this!" and then turned swiftly and seemed to regain control of himself.

He came back to where Rhianon and Bevins were standing, his eyes crafty.

"A neat trick. I'll admit it fooled me for a moment. Don't know how you got everybody to leave, but one falling rock doesn't mean a burial."

Rhianon said quietly, "Watch toward the other end of town," and again waved his hat.

This time a boulder began its plunge downward

almost before the signal was completed. Rhianon waited to speak until after its fall was completed and the dust was settling.

"The next signal starts one down heading right for the center of Coffin Rock. We'll have about three minutes to clear out."

Qualtrough said, "You don't have enough men to start those big ones moving."

"Where do you think your town people are? They're on the Rim with the settlement bunch, manning wagon jacks. They can move anything up to five tons."

Colonel Bevins said, "All you have to do is sign that release and deliver the wagons. You'll have your town; we'll have ours, and the railroad people can make their choice."

Qualtrough looked at the crumpled paper he still grasped. He said heatedly, "You win this round. There will be other times." He smoothed the paper out, his mouth forming short words Rhianon and Bevins could not hear. Something caught his attention; he threw his head up suddenly and looked past them, and a corner of his lips quirked into a smile wicked with secret triumph. He balled the paper again with a definite gesture and said, "The bargaining is going to be a bit rougher, my friends."

Rhianon turned his head, following Qualtrough's glance. Coming down the street was a party of five men. Colvig was at the head of this group. He was leading a horse with a man doubled over its saddle. The man's feet and hands were tied with heavy rope.

Colvig raised an arm, and the four men behind

him halted, making a hard and grim barrier across
that end of the street, their spread reaching from
Coffin Rock to the plank walk. And as Colvig
came closer, Rhianon instantly realized who the
man across the saddle was.

Johnny.

He never realized before that a man's heart
could actually seem to rise and lodge in his throat.
But now he felt this emptiness in his chest, and the
painful constriction of his breathing. He fought
this for a long panicky moment, making an effort
that was purely physical. He knew now what
Qualtrough's bargain would be. He could only
hope that the true identity of Johnny Minstrel was
still unknown to these men.

Colvig threw Rhianon a glance filled with hate
before speaking.

"Found this joker snooping around the wagons,
Pride. You'll recognize him."

"Johnny Minstrel," Qualtrough said.

Colvig shook his head. "We found out his real
name is somewhat different. One of the boys from
Galeyville heard his real name. His name is Johnny, all right. But his last name ain't Minstrel. It's
Rhianon."

Qualtrough turned his gaze upon Rhianon, his
smile now broad and arrogant. "Heard you had a
kid brother. Should have figured this was why you
came to Coffin Rock."

Johnny cried out, "Tell them to go to hell, Will"!

Colvig, climbing down from his horse, said
roughly, "Shut up kid!" He strode back to the led
horse and yanked Johnny from the saddle, holding
him up with one hand grasping Johnny's collar.

Qualtrough said, soft and sure and deadly, "You were talking about a bargain, I think."

Colonel Bevins let his shoulders drop. He said, "Will, don't blame yourself again."

Rhianon, feeling utterly defeated, could only slowly shake his head. There was nothing he could do. Colvig's riders still spanned the street, hands resting easily over their saddle guns. Colvig's gun arm was hidden from him, but he could tell by the backward thrust of the man's elbow that his gun was out of its holster and prodding into Johnny's side. He and Bevins and Wellington might take a few with them, but Johnny would be dead before the echoes of the first shots died away.

He cast a look up at Hell's Rim, wondering if the men up there had seen Colvig ride in, and wondered what they might be thinking, wondering if they were waiting for that next wave of his hat which would be the signal to send an avalanche of boulders crashing down upon Coffin Rock.

Qualtrough, turning to Colvig, said, "Toss him into one of the jail cells and throw the keys away." He watched Johnny go limp in Colvig's grasp, and turned his attention to Rhianon. "Make that last signal and your brother is dead. You may bury my town, but you won't have time to get him out of there."

Rhianon said in a taut voice, "I'm not the man you bargain with. You'll have to talk to Colonel Bevins."

He heard Colvig swear in an exasperated tone. He saw Johnny's knees buckle, and watched Colvig struggle to haul him to his feet. The big gunman had to holster his gun so he could use both hands.

It was then that the slow-burning hurt went out of him, and he knew what wild decision Johnny had come to. The yell rose to his throat, and he never remembered whether he uttered it or not. For he was too late.

Johnny was already erect, his bound hand furiously waving Colvig's hat above his head.

Qualtrough called, "Stop him!" but Colvig, moving with the heavy quickness of a grizzly, threw his weight against Johnny and smashed him to the ground. A rider spurred forward, whipping his Winchester from the boot and swinging it like a club. Wellington's shotgun roared, and the rider catapulted from the saddle. The horse, stirrups swinging wildly, galloped in front of Rhianon and Bevins, blocking them momentarily from Qualtrough.

Rhianon palmed his gun out, heard Wellington call out, "You other three—hold it!" Dust from the horse's hooves churned the street's middle, obscuring this view. He triggered a quickly-aimed shot toward Qualtrough, knowing instantly he had missed. And as he turned to search through the dying cloud of sun-reddened dust for Colvig, he thought he saw Qualtrough dive through the open door of the assay office. He broke through the dust's tawny waves, obsessed with a ceaseless fury, and heard Wellington's shotgun roar again and somebody's voiceless cry.

He came through his reddened shroud and saw Colvig straddled over Johnny, his gun out and his yellow teeth bared. He called, "Now is the time, Rhino!" and thrust his gun back into leather and laughed. And as Rhino Colvig turned to face him and raised his gun, he laughed again. He flicked his arm downward in a motion swift and sure. It came up again as though lifted by a blue-steel wing, silver sharp and bearing a fiery lance that swept the dust aside in great swirls and made its plummeting leap straight towards Colvig.

There was a bright-thrusting flame and a roar; and Colvig reached out as though to grasp something and then oddly turned completely around and crumpled to the street.

Rhianon shot a quick look past Johnny's still figure, then took his three quick strides and bent down to lift Johnny's head. Behind him, Third Wellington said, "Other two decided to look for better grazing."

Rhianon said, "Two?"

"Got another," Wellington said carelessly. He broke the shotgun and loaded in fresh shells.

Colonel Bevins came through the settling dust, coughing, and said, "Qualtrough's been yelling. He wants to talk."

Rhianon said, "He'll have to talk fast. We've got about one minute left. You two take Johnny to the other side of the Coffin and mount up. I'll be along."

Bevins said in a worried voice, "Will, don't take too long."

"Don't worry," said Rhianon. He turned to look toward the assay office. "Qualtrough! Time to get out of here!"

Qualtrough called back, "Give the signal not to start the rocks falling."

"No signal for that. I'm giving you a chance to get out."

"You lie, damn you! You lie! Give the signal!"

Rhianon reared a look at the top of Hell's Rim. A huge boulder balanced on its very top seemed to be swaying in the wind. A flash of sheet lightning outlined it vividly against the darkening sky, and thunder rolled down the rim's steep sides. He kept his eyes on the boulder, thinking: *It is too late now*. He heard Bevins' voice calling to him over the thunder's dying echo. He knew he couldn't make the other side of the Coffin in time; but somehow he simply couldn't leave and let Qualtrough meet a crushing death, no matter what the man had done.

He called, "Qualtrough, don't be a fool! Come on!"

The shot rang out as he saw the boulder break free. Pain streaked across his shoulder. He turned and ran directly across the street, heading for a split in the Coffin. Another shot ripped past him and richocheted from the Coffin's side. A cloud swept across the sun and plunged the town into a vast darkness. Rain pelted him as he climbed painfully up the split, its drops striking like angry seeds from the lightning's furious bloom.

He reached the top of the Coffin, hearing Qualtrough call out again. He looked down and saw the man standing in the street's middle, six-gun raised, his eyes seeing nothing but Rhianon. Behind him, down the steep slope of Hell's Rim, the boulder raced in a senseless and doubtful track, leaving a jagged scar in its wake and dislodging lesser boulders in its path. He saw the muzzle of Qualtrough's gun blossom redly, and he heard the whine of this shot as the slug glanced off the rock. He looked up briefly to see another boulder rock away from the rim and start its deadly trip downward toward Coffin Rock. Then he scrambled down the Coffin's other side, gritting his teeth when his wounded shoulder scraped against the rock.

Bevins came up to meet him, leading his horse. Wellington and Johnny were already riding out. Rhianon mounted up, and the two of them spurred off, reaching the town's outskirts just as the first boulder crashed into the Coffin. They turned in their saddles as this crashing roar engulfed them and ran its fury over them; then they bent low in their saddles and raced on, not turning again until they breasted the rise that lay a quarter of a mile from Coffin Rock.

They watched the boulders fall upon Coffin Rock, shaking its walls and making it dance upon the land. They watched Coffin Rock die beneath boulders, with the storm's flame beating against the clouds that hung over Hell's Rim. They watched the last boulder careen down the slope in wanton majesty and roll slowly into the rubble as though looking for a place to rest. A pall of dust hung over Coffin Rock; a cairn of stone marked the grave of Coffin Rock.

Third Wellington said, "Now I'll never get that middle cell cleaned out."

Rain made a never-ending tattoo upon the tent's canvas. Doc Feathers, squinting his eyes in the dull glow of a coal oil lamp, bandaged Rhianon's shoulder, saying, "Just feel lucky it wasn't your leg. You wouldn't have got to the top of that rock."

Third Wellington said, "Don't know why you waited so long."

"Couldn't see any man die that way without making a try," Rhianon answered. He turned to look at Lawney. She was standing at his other side, regarding him soberly, holding tightly to her father's arm.   Doc Feathers grunted, "Hold still, now," and started to wind the bandage. "I got your brother fixed up without any trouble. Don't you give me any."

Lawney said, "What will you do now?"

"*Quien sabe?*" Rhianon said. "What is there left to do?"

"We'll need good horses," Colonel Bevins said quietly. "Lots of good land here for a horse ranch."

"That's a thought," Rhianon said. "That's a mighty good thought." He put his gaze fully upon Lawney Bevins and said gravely, "Half expected you to come dashing up with your wagon again. Where were you when I needed you?"

Her glance met his steadily. There was a sparkle of lantern's light in her eyes.

"From now on," she said, "whenever you need me, I'll be there."

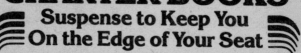